~ Acclaim for J. C. Owens ~

Praise for *Taken*

"*Taken* was my surprise hit of the year. ...[A] rollercoaster ride of awesome. Landon and Kirith are like molten hot lava thrown on your skin. Yes people, it burns so good."

—Darien Moya for *Pants Off Reviews*

~ Look for these titles from J. C. Owens ~

Now Available from Etopia Press

Taken
Wings 2: Dominion of the Eth
Wishes
Out of the Darkness
The Ice Prince

Also as J. C. McGuire

The Ascension
The Gloaming
The Conquered
The Triumph

Out of the Darkness

Taken Book Two

J. C. Owens

etopia
press

Etopia Press
1643 Warwick Ave., #124
Warwick, RI 02889
http://www.etopia-press.net

OUT OF THE DARKNESS

Print ISBN: 978-1-941692-46-2
Digital ISBN: 978-1-940223-79-7

First Etopia Press electronic publication: January 2014

First Etopia Press print publication: January 2015

~ Dedication ~

For all those readers who asked repeatedly for a story involving Enzo and Chase. Hope I do them justice…

And to Matt, for some truly exemplary editing! You make me sound good. :)

Chapter One

Chase fastened the seat belt with shaking fingers, then curled into his seat, a wary eye fixed on the man beside him.

The helicopter rose with smooth ease, and Chase's companion lifted a long-fingered hand in farewell to the small group of family and friends below.

He shivered. He had grown used to his position on the island, serving as unofficial companion to the convalescing Kirith Martinelli. Now, Kirith was back with his lover, Landon, and his daughter, Laura. Chase was not needed.

He shivered once more, wrapping his arms around himself in a futile search for comfort. This was the first time he had been alone with his rescuer, and the power emanating from the man made him want to fling himself to the floor and offer obeisance to lessen the degree of punishment he was sure to receive. For them to be sitting side by side, as though they were equals, made Chase tense and anxious. This went against every bit of training he'd ever received, but he had discovered that his new master frowned upon any of his former actions, even to refusing sexual favors. Chase had tried numerous times to offer his body, but to his increasing fear, his new master seemed impervious to his charms. That couldn't mean anything positive. Sex was all he was good for. If his master did not want that, he was sure to get rid of him, and he would be back in the hell he had been rescued from.

"Chase."

He froze, shaken from his tortured musings. Immediately he bowed his head and tried to curl in his seat enough to convey respect and obedience.

A huff of breath told him his actions had not found favor.

"Chase, look at me."

With difficulty he looked up, unable to make his gaze go higher than lips drawn into a thin line. It was forbidden, under pain of beating, ever to meet a master's eyes. The closest he could come was focusing on the lean Italian nose and thinking how utterly beautiful his new master was.

"My brother tells me that you think I will dispose of you as soon as I arrive back on the mainland."

Chase's breath ceased altogether. How could Kirith have betrayed him?

He cupped Chase's chin with his lean hand and tilted his head up just slightly so he had to meet that cool gaze. "I told you back when we rescued both you and Laura that you were with me now. I meant that. That does not mean that I am going to discard you when you are not convenient." Complete conviction resounded in that deep, low tone. Chase believed what his master said was true. At least it was for now.

"Yes, master," he whispered.

A sigh this time. "I have told you before. You call me Enzo. Or if that is too difficult, Mr. Martinelli."

He nodded, flushing. He had forgotten — again. It just was so hard to go against his training. "Yes, sir."

Enzo shook his head, but his face seemed to soften slightly, a rare sight indeed. "Close enough." The stern tone returned. "Don't call me master again. I am nothing like the bastards who treated you like a living sex toy." The distaste in the words made him cringe. His mas — Mr. Martinelli was right. He was nothing like those other men. Enzo was so much more, like a hero of old. He had rescued Chase from hell—and then kept him. No one had ever wanted to keep him before. He looked up adoringly, wishing he could express his feelings in some fashion that didn't disgust Mr. Martinelli.

Those brown eyes searched his expression for long moments, then Enzo sighed again, patting his cheek gently before releasing his face.

"I have work to do. Just relax. You don't have to do anything, be anything. Just watch the view, all right?"

Chase nodded, overwhelmed with the kindness he was being shown. It was as if he were a person. Did Mr. Martinelli see him as a person? He wasn't even sure what that meant. He saw himself as less than nothing; that had been drilled into him from a child, from the day of his first training session. What did his rescuer see that was so much more?

He chewed at his thumbnail, watching Enzo from beneath the fringe of his hair.

The Martinelli had a headset on and began barking orders to someone, the muted roar of the helicopter seeming little impediment.

Chase sighed softly. Enzo wasn't quite real to him, more like a fictional character who had swept out of nowhere to save a tortured soul.

The sheer beauty of the man made him almost more than believable: the short black hair so perfectly styled, the harsh, chiseled face that so seldom showed any expression, the brown eyes that seemed almost black in most lights. His body was powerful, broad-shouldered, slim-hipped, his beautiful dark skin showing his Italian ancestry clearly. He had the leashed energy of a predator, hyper-aware of his surroundings, but content to relax until something drew that intimidating gaze. This man was no one to cross. He had defeated Chase's former master, Marcello—killed him to save Kirith. This was not a gentle man, but in all Chase's life, he had known nothing but violence. That Enzo had shown him a form of caring beyond that was hard to fathom.

Chase could have stared at him all day, but he knew that could only bring about irritation in the end, so he reluctantly turned his attention to the window beside him, watching the sea below with increasing fascination. He'd never had the opportunity to see out during the last flight to the island, so this was his first view of the sea from such a vantage point.

He felt so much better physically that it was hard to believe this was not all a mirage. He had enough to eat, and he slept in a clean, fresh bed. He was never required to give himself sexually, although that part gave him great anxiety. Perhaps with time, his mas — Mr. Martinelli — might come to see him as attractive enough for sexual use, but until then, he would strive to account himself in any way possible.

He struggled to believe that here — at last — was hope.

* * *

Enzo's assistant, Raymond, looked up as Chase entered the outer office, his cold face softening somewhat as he took in Chase's nervousness.

"Mr. Martinelli is waiting for you." He gestured to the door of the inner sanctum, and Chase nodded jerkily, sidling past him, always nervous of the stern demeanor Raymond exuded. The man was good at his job, but he was impossible to read — even more so than Enzo's head of security, Sergei. Chase always found himself tongue-tied in his presence.

He raised his hand and knocked, swallowing hard as he felt Raymond's eyes on his back.

"Come in."

Shaking with nerves, his fingers spasmed as he turned the

doorknob and entered the cool, dark sanctuary that was Enzo Martinelli's office. The man himself looked up slowly from his work, his finger marking where he was reading, his eyes pinning Chase to the spot. For long moments they were frozen in tableau. He took a deep, quivering breath. Being this close to the man he admired so deeply made thinking almost beyond his current capabilities.

At last Enzo sighed. Chase felt his stomach drop. What had he done now to disappoint his savior?

"Sit. We need to talk."

With dragging steps, he approached and sank into the huge chair indicated, feeling almost swallowed by its size.

He stared at the floor, pleating his fingers together with nervous intensity, biting his lip until the abused flesh bled, as it did so often.

Enzo reached out his hand and tugged the lip free of his teeth. Chase looked up into tired brown eyes, feeling guilt at bringing this man yet more disturbance. He was such a burden.

"You don't need to be afraid here." The words held the ring of repeated utterance. "No one would dare hurt you in the slightest. Do you think I am not capable of protecting you?"

Chase gasped in horror and shook his head wildly. Mr. Martinelli was so powerful. There was nothing he couldn't do. He had never thought—

"Stop panicking." Enzo's voice was sharp, snapping him out of his fearful musings. "Look at me."

Chase looked, fighting to keep his expression normal and not allow his infatuation to shine through, as he knew it so often did.

"I've summoned you today to ask why you refuse to speak to Peter. He is very good at what he does. Look at how he helped Kirith." Enzo sighed, rubbing the bridge of his nose. "Why will you not work with him? He can help you. Do you want to stay locked in fear?"

Chase shook his head again fervently. God, he didn't want to stay in the trap that engulfed him, but…

"I have nothing to talk about, sir. He wants to know what I'm thinking, feeling. How can that be important? It's never been important before."

The Martinelli leaned forward and laid a strong hand upon Chase's jaw. The warmth made Chase press into the touch, craving the contact. "It was not important before because those bastards were trying to break you. There is so much pain inside you, just like there was in Kirith. The wound has to be lanced, the pain purged. You cannot go on until you face yourself."

"I hate myself, sir," he whispered. Tears brimmed at the corner of his eyes, despite his fight to control his emotion. "I don't want to talk about myself. I just want what I am to go away, so I can become someone else."

Enzo leaned closer, cradling his face in both hands, forcing him to meet serious eyes. "I like who you are. I don't want you to change into someone else. Can you heal for me if you cannot do it for yourself?"

He blinked away the tears and nodded. He would do anything for his savior, and if this was what Mr. Martinelli wanted, then he would achieve it, no matter the cost. It was little enough to give to a man who had gifted him a new life. If Mr. Martinelli thought he was worth saving—worth keeping as he was, scars and all—then maybe there was something worthwhile within after all. He couldn't conceive what the Martinelli saw, but the man was surely wiser than he was. Therefore, Chase didn't have to decide anything about himself at all. He just had to obey. Had to please his idol.

"I will speak to Mr. —Peter—" He managed even to use the man's name, not his title, and felt quite proud of himself for the distinction.

Enzo nodded, perhaps picking up that small nuance of success. "That is all I can ask of you. I might have freed you from that room, but it is up to you to free yourself from what lays within you." He smiled, and Chase's heart pounded in reaction.

He would do anything to earn that smile again.

Chapter Two

Two Years Later

Enzo woke suddenly, his private phone ringing in his ear. He snarled silently, snatching it from the bedside table and stabbing the touchscreen with a finger.

"What? It is four o'clock in the fucking morning," he snapped, murder in the tone.

"We have him." The tone was pure satisfaction, and Enzo found himself suddenly and completely awake.

Landon, his brother's lover, had been keeping tabs on the search for the men who had kidnapped Kirith and his daughter Laura on that horrific night. Although Landon would not leave Kirith's side for a moment now, he had been adamant about being involved in the manhunt. Such infamy and betrayal would not be ignored. All of Landon's buddies in his tactical ops team had aided in the effort, and Enzo had offered unlimited funds in the quest to find the last links in the horror that his brother had undergone.

Kirith knew nothing of what was transpiring, and they kept it from him with the best of intentions. Lethal though Kirith could be, he did not have the ruthlessness of his brother, and his state of health was still a concern after what he had undergone.

He and Landon would see it through and bear Kirith's anger

afterward if he should learn of it.

They had caught and eliminated all the vermin. Only the last, the biggest of the betrayers, was still at large.

"Where?" Pleasure and fury shot up his spine as he sat bolt upright against the ornate carved headboard.

With vicious satisfaction in his tone, Landon named a small town in northern Florida. "You'll take care of it?"

Enzo knew how much the younger man longed to be in on this revenge. "It will be done swiftly."

"Not too swiftly?" Landon's tone held all the fury he could not release.

"No." Enzo smiled, cruel anticipation rising within him. "I will see it lasts enough for us both."

* * *

Jason woke in degrees, slowly and groggily becoming aware of his surroundings. It took long moments for his mind to take in the fact he knelt upon a cold floor, his arms chained above his head, and when those facts finally came to light, his mind beginning to function, he felt his whole body freeze in terror.

He blinked, trying to clear his vision, then wished he hadn't. He whispered a prayer beneath his breath, pulling futilely at the chains.

A few feet away, relaxed back in the chair, the Devil sat with a wineglass in hand.

Jason's breath caught, his heart pounding in terror. Dear God…

The man simply watched him: cold, brown eyes almost black in the stark light of the florescent bulbs. Dressed simply but elegantly in black dress pants and pristine white shirt, he seemed out of place in the dank room, the peeling paint a strange backdrop to his male beauty.

He sipped the wine, never taking his eyes from Jason,

absolutely no expression on that handsome face. No hint of malice or menace showed in his expression, but malevolence radiated from his very presence like some living, breathing angel of death. Behind him, another man stood in the shadows, cold expression barely visible.

Raymond.

Jason trembled, his gaze pinned beneath that dark, fathomless stare. He'd thought he'd escaped. Thought he had been so clever, even when all the others had been caught and had died horribly if rumors were true.

He felt despair well within him, a glimpse of his own foolishness.

One didn't escape Enzo Martinelli.

Enzo carefully placed the wineglass upon the small table, the tiny sound jarring Jason's nerves. Raymond stepped forward to fill it with the swift efficiency he was so noted for. Enzo rose soundlessly with the grace of a predator. He reached to his waist and then flicked his hand, the blade opening with a faint snick, the edge gleaming in the light.

Jason felt warm wetness seeping into his pants and a whimper escaping his throat.

"It wasn't me! I swear to God it wasn't me! They conned me into it, told me Kirith and the girl wouldn't be harmed! I swear!"

The blade kissed his cheek, so sharp it took moments for him to realize that he was actually cut, that blood was running down his neck, hot and thick.

"God isn't listening, Jason. He knows you. He knows what you have done, and I think he will be looking elsewhere for worthy people to save today, hmm?" The Martinelli's voice was soft and rich, almost gentle.

A sob burst from his throat. He opened tear-wet eyes. "Please…"

The knife flashed, and the other cheek opened.

"Did my little niece plead with you as you took her from her home? As you took her father and delivered him to Marcello, knowing what would happen to him?" The voice was eerily calm.

Jason shuddered. "It was a mistake, forgive me."

He raised one dark eyebrow, his eyes growing colder. "A mistake? Yes, it was, Jason. You betrayed me. You harmed my family." He straightened up, flicking blood away before passing it to Raymond. The aide produced a cloth from his pocket and swept it across the blade with brisk efficiency before snapping it closed with a flick of his wrist. Enzo accepted the blade back, sitting down at the table and picking up his glass once more.

He swirled the liquid, inhaling deeply. "You did well, Raymond. This vintage does great justice to the vintner."

Raymond nodded, corking the bottle with care. "I think I might order a few more bottles, if you approve."

Enzo took a sip, letting it linger upon his tongue for long moments before swallowing. "I very much approve."

"Trent," he called then, and Jason began to fight his chains, crying out as the door opened and a large form limped through. His former captain. The man he had tried to kill when Kirith had been taken.

Lips drew back from white teeth in a feral grin.

"Hello, Jason. Long time no see. I've been waiting to talk to you." Trent motioned with his left hand, and four other men strode into the room, all of them frighteningly familiar to Jason. "Remember us? The ones you tried to kill, the ones you betrayed? You killed seven of us that night; seven lives you owe us."

Trent looked over at Enzo, and the Martinelli nodded.

Trent grinned. "It's going to be a long night, Jason. Too bad you won't see morning."

The men moved forward.

Enzo glanced at Raymond, but his assistant shook his head when his boss gestured toward Jason. Watching would give him enough satisfaction it seemed. Enzo turned back, lips slowly curling into a terrifyingly satisfied smile.

* * *

Chase heaved a deep sigh, slamming the car door behind him as he struggled to hold all his books. His old Jetta looked like a country cousin parked amidst the Mercedes and Escalades, with Enzo's Audi R8 sneering at it from its own place of honor near the front door.

His heart raced a little at sight of the beautiful car.

Enzo was home then.

He'd been gone some three weeks attending business somewhere in Florida, and Chase knew better than to question where or how long his guardian might be.

Enzo was gentle with him, but he also demanded total respect and compliance in return, and the members of the household knew to keep any curiosity completely hidden. Their boss had no patience for mistakes or less than perfect work. Loyalty was paramount and not up for negotiation. The slightest hint otherwise was a fatal blunder.

In return, the Martinelli knew every person on the estate, every member of their family, every minute detail of their lives, and he saw to it that they were cared for and protected with his name and his resources.

The staff loved him and feared him in the same breath.

Chase merely loved him.

He'd gone through too much in his young life to begin to fear the man who was his hero, his savior. His only fear was that one day his guardian would see him for the tainted soul he was and cast him out from his presence.

That would be the end of days.

He couldn't remember how old he had been when he first

started living on the streets, when he had first sold his body. He had dim memories of a mother too far gone in drugs and alcohol to feed her child or to care what he did; it was a vague and surreal thing, as though she had never really existed at all. Amazingly, he had avoided the drugs, more out of the need to eat than any real intention, although he had seen far too much of what they did and where people ended up under their influence. He probably would have ended up just another drug statistic if Marcello had not found him and taken him for his entertainment. In some ways, he owed the man. In other ways, his mind was forever scarred by what he had undergone while in those cruel hands.

He was drug-free, but a mental wreck.

It was ironic that he now lived with the head of the Martinelli family, kings of the drug trade. If his acquaintances could see him now — living in the lap of luxury — they would think him the luckiest bastard who ever existed. It was like a fairy tale or a movie. The prostitute falling in love with a rich mobster.

If only it was returned.

He sighed a little wistfully, wending his way through the multitude of vehicles.

If there were this many people here, then Enzo was probably caught up in meetings.

Still, there was hope to see him at dinner. Enzo always liked to know how Chase's day had gone, how his schooling was coming. He had insisted on him going to the local college to work on finishing high school courses so that he could choose a career.

It had been made very plain indeed that he would *not* be joining the family in any illegal activities.

Chase was touched that Enzo wanted to keep him from the seamier side of life, but it seemed a little late for that. Still, he would do anything to make the older man proud, and if going to college and making something of himself was the way, then he would do it gladly.

He was proving to be more intelligent than he would have given himself credit for, and it was beginning to give him a modicum of confidence.

Two years of psychological therapy had not hurt either.

He was beginning to feel less like a ragged excuse for a soul and more like a person, one who had a chance in life now and should grasp it with both hands…and thank God and Enzo in the doing.

The front door swung open at his approach. He sighed with relief and shifted the books in his arms. He did not have a hand to work with at the moment. Rafe, one of the younger bodyguards, cousin to a close friend of Sergei's, grinned at him. He was only twenty-five, two years older than Chase and not as standoffish as the other guards. Chase smiled back. Rafe was beautiful. But he felt nothing when he looked at that perfect body. His heart was already taken. Hopelessly.

Rafe grabbed half the books, pretending to groan under the weight.

"You don't need to work out, Chase. I never realized learning was so damn heavy." He staggered along, some of the other nearby bodyguards rolling their eyes at his performance, especially Sergei, the head of security, whom Rafe lived to annoy.

Chase chuckled. No matter how down he might get, Rafe knew exactly how to bring him out of it.

Rafe was a friend. Possibly he wanted to be more than that, but Chase did not want him to be hurt, to realize he could only ever be second best.

Rafe tossed the books down on the kitchen table, and the housekeeper, Ms. Granger, turned to look at him with patent disapproval that softened as soon as she saw Chase.

Chase did not really understand why, but it seemed that he was a favorite with many of the staff. They looked after him, tried to keep his spirits up, and, in Ms. Granger's case, fed him until he exploded.

"I made you the chicken lasagna you like so much. Just ten more minutes."

She looked a little harassed today, and the sound of laughter beyond the double doors of the vast kitchen certainly explained why.

He raised a brow. "That's an awfully noisy meeting."

Ms. Granger frowned, casting a glance filled with loathing toward the ruckus.

"*She…*" the single word spoke volumes, "planned a party for Mr. Martinelli. Ordered caterers, as though I cannot cook."

He clenched his fingers on the table edge, trying to keep his face neutral enough. The rest of the staff disliked Stacey as it was. He did not need to add fuel to the fire.

"A party for what?"

"Who knows? The stage of the moon perhaps?" Ms. Granger's acid tongue gave an edge to the words. Rafe coughed, obviously hiding a laugh.

Chase frowned at him. The last thing they needed was to set Ms. Granger on a rampage. People suffered for days after such an event, and usually it was Enzo who had to calm things down.

"She's just trying to—"

"She is just trying to get a ring on her finger. I used to think Mr. Martinelli was too smart for such tactics, but lately, I don't know." Her disapproval was evident.

Chase's stomach clenched. His indrawn breath was shaky at best.

"Where is he?" He was proud that the longing he felt was absent from those simple words.

"In the pool." Ms. Granger almost spit the words, and she turned back to the kitchen counter with dark dislike painted clearly in her expression.

His eyebrows rose. "The pool? Enzo never has time to—"

"Apparently he has time for *her*. Foolish man. I have half a mind to tell him…"

Chase laid a hand on her arm, ever the peacemaker. "He's been pretty tense these last few months. Maybe he just needs to unwind a little. This might be a good thing."

She hesitated, then half turned to him, looking up into his eyes with a searching gaze that saw things far too clearly for his peace of mind. Her anger seemed to drain away into something more weary and worn.

She took a hand and reached up to tuck a strand of rebellious hair behind his ear. "He is looking for something that is right here."

He tilted his head questioningly, but she just patted his cheek and turned back to her work.

"I just know that if she becomes mistress here, I am going elsewhere." Her words were punctuated by the whack of the knife on the board, making even Rafe look somewhat nervous.

Chase gave her a hug from the back, kissing her cheek.

"He would never find such a talented cook as you, Ms. Granger. I would probably pine away for your food, and you would have to feel so guilty."

She tried not to smile, but smacked him lightly, thankfully with the hand that *didn't* hold the knife.

"Get on with you, boy. Pine away, indeed. Why don't you go out and swim? It might be the only chance to actually encounter himself in the pool, and I know you enjoy the water."

He nodded obediently. Normally he would have avoided the party like the plague, since he hated elaborate get-togethers where the guests were drunk or high as kites. But right now, he missed Enzo terribly, not to mention this would be a rare chance to see him in swimming trunks.

Fuel for jacking off for a long time to come.

What magazine could possibly compare?

Decision made, he sprinted out of the kitchen. If he did not hurry…

He changed into his swimming trunks in record time, pulling a black T-shirt on as well, not wishing to go out amongst strangers half nude. He drew a deep breath as he went down the stairs silently in bare feet. It was going to be hard to face all these people, especially if a lot of them were men. He had come a long way since his experiences with Marcello, but his therapist had made it very clear that the mental scars would always be there. All he could do was try to understand himself and his reactions, to gain control. And he had, with a mixture of determination and strength he would never have thought he possessed. For the first time in his life, with Enzo looking after him, he had felt safe enough to try to understand himself, to feel like maybe he was worth trying for.

He had a long way to go—he held no illusions of that—but he had come far already and Enzo had made it perfectly clear that that was something to be proud of.

Chase had to believe him, right?

He passed through the huge double doors that delineated the private areas of the family from the ornate parts of the villa that hosted outsiders. He blinked at the array of people before threading his way through their ranks. Most were standing, talking, and laughing, drinks in hand, the smell of marijuana heavy in the air.

This close, he could see the dilated pupils of many of the guests, and he steered clear of those people, not wanting to incite any weird reactions from them. Obviously more than pot was being passed around. Most of them merely glanced at him, then away, seeing only a young man of no particular importance in their world. Chase was grateful and kept his gaze away from any specific person. Some men he recognized here, and their tempers were something to avoid.

He could hear splashing from the pool before he could actually see it through the bodies standing in his way, and he caught

Stacey's high-pitched giggle that always made him grit his teeth. When he finally managed to get to the edge, he noticed the hungry looks on several of the nearby women as they watched someone in the water, and at least two men had the same expression.

He could not blame them.

Enzo sliced through the water with the same precise power that he displayed in everything he did. He was doing laps, but without true speed, merely a lazy stretching of muscles as his restlessness drove him to move.

Chase drew a shivering breath into his lungs, eyes tracing every line of that beautiful body with a longing that made his chest ache.

Enzo reached the end and dived, pushing off, the muscles of his legs clearly delineated for a moment before he began swimming again. He seemed oblivious to everyone around him, as though he were utterly alone. Even those guests who were in the water, floating lazily by the sides, were ignored.

Chase shot a quick, guilty glance to the far side of the pool, where Stacey was holding court with admirers and friends, her perfect body artfully arranged on the chaise lounge. His lips twisted. Far be it for her actually to get wet. Stacey always seemed like one not to let anything ruin her perfect veneer or to participate in anything that might show her as anything approaching mortal.

He returned his attention to Enzo, his heart quickening as he realized Enzo had changed course and was heading directly for him.

He held his ground, hands twisting in the towel, wishing he could be cooler and calmer around the object of his affection.

Enzo reached the side of the pool and raised one hand to rake back his thick, black hair, looking up at him with a slow smile that made Chase shiver with longing. That smile did the most amazing things to his stomach, making it tie in knots while his heart sped up.

The smile itself was rare enough to be greatly treasured, and right now, it held a certain fondness, a slight opening for him that few received.

It meant more to Chase than any amount of money. That this intensely private man had accepted him—let him into his inner circle—was heady indeed.

Those dark eyes moved down his body, lingering on his shorts for moment. Before Chase could realize what was happening, Enzo lunged up and caught him around the waist, dragging him into the water.

He barely had the forethought to suck in a breath before he struck the water's surface.

A certain madness overcame him, and he twisted like an eel out of Enzo's hold before turning to drag the older man under the water with him.

Enzo did not even seem to resist, and through the clear water of the pool, Chase saw the grin that denoted warfare.

He lunged for the surface, gasping and sputtering, managing a few breaths before the Martinelli was on him again. They rolled like two otters, a playfulness in Enzo's manner that few would have associated with him.

Chase gave up the fight—well, it was give up or drown—laughing so hard he could scarcely breathe.

"I give, geez, I give already!" He folded his arms over the edge of the pool, panting and coughing, wiping back his hair with one hand as he glared at Enzo. "My school marks are going to be useless if you kill me before I graduate."

Enzo laughed out loud, a rare event that made heads turn, as though everyone had not been watching them discretely anyway. Enzo Martinelli was not known to have a lighter side. To see it displayed so blatantly would be fuel for gossip for a long time to come, no doubt.

Enzo floated beside him, arms folded as Chase's were, elbow to elbow on the ornate pool edge. He still grinned slightly; his deep brown eyes alight, and for once free of the shadows that denoted his darker nature.

Chase tried not to focus on the drops of water that gleamed upon that dark Italian skin, trickled down that harsh, handsome face. He tried to push aside the need and want that had hardened his body in very inconvenient places. The Martinelli could never know that the pathetic little waif he had rescued was madly, completely in love with him. It would be the final humiliation for Chase.

Such a powerful man, and so beautiful, had many panting after him. He did not need yet another person lusting for him. Their relationship had slowly molded into a friendship of sorts, a guardian/ward type of bond that meant more to him than anything else.

Enzo cared. It may have started in necessity, not knowing quite what to do with Chase when he had rescued him, but it had ended in this, whatever *this* might be labeled. Enzo's niece, Laura, might have started it all, with her refusal to let Chase out of her sight after their mutual imprisonment, but the Martinelli could have discreetly shuffled Chase off to a private treatment facility after Laura returned to her father, Kirith, and his lover, Landon. It would have been what most men would have done — a damaged young man on their hands, of no blood ties whatsoever.

That Enzo had kept him had always confused Chase, but his idol had made it very plain that he was here for the long term, as long as he wished. There had been no doubts about that, no gray areas for him to worry about or build to epic proportions with his innate lack of self-worth.

As long as he wished — forever sounded pretty damn good.

His thoughts fled as Enzo hoisted himself with athletic ease from the pool, water sluicing down over that powerful form, shining with a silver tinge in the sun's light. Chase had to force his jaw closed, fight back the drool that wanted to form.

So damn beautiful…and so unattainable.

Enzo offered a hand, and Chase reached up to grasp it, trying to imprint all these moments upon his mind's eye so he could take them out later and examine each with the reverence it deserved.

The grip of that powerful hand, the way the muscles of the arm delineated as he was pulled up and out of the water with little effort, the feel of those long fingers wrapped around his own… All these were gems beyond price.

Enzo shook his head, before turning away to grasp a pristinely white towel that lay over a nearby chair.

He toweled his hair, but did not attempt to dry himself elsewhere, simply wrapping the towel around his waist, the white stark against his bronzed skin. Chase followed his motions with his own, though he quickly toweled his torso enough that he could put his T-shirt back on, his modesty appeased.

Enzo laid a hand on his shoulder, his face more closed now than it had been in the pool, as though he had remembered they had an avid audience.

"I hear Ms. Granger has made your favorite dish. *Noi mangeremo, sì*? And you will tell me of your day. Then shall I return to the party."

Chase nodded, shooting a trepidant look to the nearby chaise that held Stacey. She was watching them, a hint of anger in her expression, something that chased away her blatant beauty and made her seem older, more grasping.

"My love, you cannot mean to leave our party. I have food ready. Surely even he is capable of eating alone, is he not?"

Enzo had been listening to her courteously enough, but her last words made his eyes narrow, the shadows flare to life with frightening speed.

He went to her, a half smile upon his lips, and she smiled back victoriously. He bent to kiss her, then held her head in his hands so only she could see what lay in his eyes. Only she and Chase, who was nearest, could hear his words.

"Do not think ever to control me, my lovely one. Despite what you hold for me, that would be a very, very large mistake, hmm?"

Her body stiffened. She managed to nod, never taking her suddenly fearful eyes from Enzo's, like a rabbit huddling before a wolf.

He kissed her forehead and released her, his expression pleasant and relaxed once more, as though the incident had never occurred.

"I shall return soon, *sì*?"

Stacey nodded again, obviously struggling to control her expression so that the guests would not realize her faux pas. She had stepped over a line and received a small rake of the dragon's claws for the trespass.

Chase wanted to feel sorry for her, but she had best learn now, before…

He followed in Enzo's wake, clenching his teeth.

Dear God, please don't let them get married. He couldn't imagine having to live here and watch Enzo love someone else. It was hard enough now, though Stacey rarely seemed to visit. It always seemed to be Enzo going elsewhere to meet her. Whether that was her choice or Enzo's remained to be seen, but he couldn't imagine the Martinelli going out of his way for anyone, much less answer a woman's beck and call. Therefore it had to be Enzo's will that kept her from the villa, and he could only be grateful.

Enzo gestured to Raymond, and the PA gave a nod. He would circulate, keep things in line until his boss returned. Chase shivered. Sometimes he felt that Raymond was far more dangerous than Sergei and the others, if for no other reason than people underestimated him. Of an age with Enzo, short, slim, with pale gray eyes and a pleasant—if not handsome—face, he had a talent for blending into the background, something that must be of great use to the Martinelli. Raymond was his second set of eyes and ears. From what Chase had overheard, the man was a martial arts expert, had even taken Sergei down now and then. Chase always felt inadequate in the man's presence, though Raymond had never indicated he disliked Chase in the least.

He was relieved when they passed out of sight of the party and into the kitchen. Ms. Granger looked over her shoulder, her eyes lighting when she saw them.

Enzo laid a kiss upon her cheek before seating himself at the small table. "I hear there is lasagna to be had?"

Ms. Granger bloomed, pleasure radiating from her smiling face.

"There is, Mr. Martinelli. I made it for Chase. But I thought you would be eating at the party."

Enzo made a dismissing gesture with one hand. "And miss your lasagna? Ms. Granger, I am not a foolish man."

She shook her head at him, still smiling. "No, sir. I'll just put some garlic bread on. It will only be a few minutes."

Enzo leaned back in the chair, the picture of relaxation. "Do not worry. The young one and I have much time."

Chase felt his muscles unwinding as he took a seat opposite Enzo. So, it seemed he would not be rushing back to the party. Whether it was because he was punishing Stacey or because he simply wanted to stay was hard to tell.

Either way, he had Enzo practically to himself, and he treasured every moment.

"*Cosi, ragazzo mio*, how was school?"

Chase tried to look positive, but his eyes gave him away as always, and Enzo frowned.

"Most of my classes are great," he hurried to clarify. "It's just my English teacher is being…odd. My marks are falling."

Enzo leaned forward, crossing his forearms on the table, his dark eyes intent. "Odd? Who is this teacher?"

"Mr. Wayson. He was fine at the beginning of the year and then..." Chase paused, wondering if it was wise to speak of any of this. He blushed at his own thoughts.

Enzo watched him with that motionless intensity that was so unnerving.

"Chase?" The tone held command.

"He was OK and then he found out I was..." he choked off, looking anywhere but his mentor. "Gay. He found out I was gay."

Chase wondered if he could just slide under the table. Surely Enzo wouldn't be disgusted. His own brother, Kirith, had chosen a man for his life partner. But still, to admit this in front of the man he so desired...

The Martinelli raised an eyebrow. "And this should affect your marks in what way, *i giovani*? You are telling me this man marks work based on sexual preference? Have you complained to the head of the school?"

"I tried. He just shrugged, said that they would look into it. They offered to switch classes, but it would not fit with the rest of my schedule."

He saw the look in Enzo's eyes. "But it's fine. I'm almost finished, and my marks were high enough in the beginning that I should be able to pass, and that is all that matters." He didn't know if he was trying to persuade himself or his guardian.

"I have read your essays. They are good—better than good. If you were not interested in architecture, I would say you could have a career in writing, *si*? Therefore your work should be graded as to its own worth, not what your teacher deems through his own prejudice."

Chase fiddled with the silverware. "Are you OK with..." he waved one hand rather helplessly, "what I told you?" His heart felt like it could pound out of his chest. If Enzo rejected him...

The Martinelli gave a small smile, tilting his head as he viewed Chase's flushed features. "That you are *omosessuale*? I have known that for some time. It is hardly a shock and certainly nothing to judge you on. Did you think I would do otherwise?"

"No, not with Kirith and everything, but...I'm not really a Martinelli." He bowed his head, unable to look at his face.

"You are a member of this family if I say you are." Enzo's tone held no compromise or doubt.

Chase tried to smile but it was tenuous. "I keep thinking you are going to see the real me, and then you'll toss me out on my ass."

Enzo tsk-tsked, but there was a small smile at the corner of his lips. "We have gone over this. You are one of us now, there will be no tossing."

He had to grin at that, finally finding the courage to look up. Enzo's expression held no difference than before, no judgment.

"Thank you, even though that seems totally not enough for what you do for me."

Enzo nodded, not trying to shrug off his statement. "I do not need gratitude. I only need to see you start your life. That will be your gift to me."

He nodded. "I won't let you down."

Enzo's eyes seemed to soften more than Chase could ever remember seeing, except perhaps with Kirith and Laura. "I know you won't."

Those few words buoyed Chase's confidence as nothing else could. Enzo believed in him and had accepted he was gay without any sort of prejudice. The day seemed brighter already.

Ms. Granger bustled over, laying down generous helpings of lasagna and slices of freshly baked bread before each of them. "*Grazie.*" Enzo smiled, picking up his fork and digging in with evident enjoyment. Chase had to force himself to pay attention to his own meal; his fascination with each and every thing that Enzo did was bordering on the extreme. He tried to act normally, to keep everything he was feeling off his face.

"Stacey says she is carrying my child."

The casual words dropped like stones into the room. There was a crash from the kitchen, and Chase choked on his mouthful, having to grab a napkin as he coughed helplessly, eyes watering.

Dear God. He couldn't have heard that. *Please don't let it be true.*

He took a deep drink of juice, then sat trying to breathe, watching through incredulous eyes as Enzo continued to eat with calm aplomb, as though he hadn't just changed the world, or at least this corner of it.

The potent silence from the kitchen said more than words ever could.

"She is pregnant?" Chase almost whispered, and he clenched his fingers under the tabletop, desperately attempting to hide his horror.

Enzo shrugged. "She says she is."

He had to ask, to find out the worst.

"You're going to marry her then?" He could hardly believe how steady his voice was.

Enzo finished his mouthful and wiped his lips with a napkin, a frown settling on his brows, more of thought than true anger.

"No, not yet. Once the child is born and it is proven mine, then we shall see."

He found himself able to breathe again. Surely something would come along to change the course of this travesty. Enzo deserved to be loved — and Stacey loved nothing but his wealth and power. Why did Enzo not see that?

The answer was clear enough, certainly so to Chase, who had studied Enzo so diligently. Over two years, it had become greatly evident to him that Enzo had no idea what love truly was, certainly not between lovers. The Martinelli loved his family — Kirith and Laura — with deep intensity, but even then, Chase didn't believe that Enzo understood what it was he was experiencing. There had been a parade of women during his stay, but only Stacey had become more than a one-night stand. Enzo was generous enough to his lovers, with everything besides his heart. Even with Stacey, Chase had seen nothing but a kind of tolerant amusement, nothing of true connection.

He wanted so much more for this man. He wanted him to be loved for who he was, not what he was. Who else was going to give that but Chase himself?

But such feelings had to be kept under wraps. If Enzo even suspected, things would become so uncomfortable that he would have no choice but to move out.

That scenario was both attractive and horrifying. Attractive because he would be free of this unending obsession, with the chance to create a normal life. Horrifying because he couldn't imagine his existence without Enzo nearby.

He laid his aching head on one hand. He was fucking hooped.

Chapter Three

Chase was a complicated little package, Enzo mused as he finished his lasagna. He was well aware that Stacey and the boy did not get along and that was one of the major bones of contention between him and the woman who could end up being his wife. It was why he seldom invited Stacey to the villa. Tanglewood was Chase's home; he should feel safe here. It was important to him on a level he did not truly understand. The boy had been through too much already; he needed security above all, and Enzo was going to provide that security, see the boy safe so that he had a foundation to step from in his life.

As for Stacey—she was beginning to become a problem, and if she continued, she would be finding herself sequestered somewhere far away until the child was born. He considered the notion for some time. He was well aware she wanted him for his money and position; he expected nothing else of a woman. But that she was growing possessive and hostile toward Chase…

That he would never permit.

He did not trust Stacey as a stable influence whatsoever, but she was good-looking enough and had a certain cold intelligence that would mesh well with his own. The children created would be perfect for governing the family.

He sat back in his chair and considered the matter for some

time before his eyes fixed upon Chase's woebegone expression as he poked at his food.

He smiled at the boy's simplicity.

"She is not moving in here. Do not worry. I would not inflict her moodiness upon you."

Chase looked up, hope evident in his eyes. "Would you still live here though?"

Enzo finished his juice and set aside the glass.

"I have no intention of ever living with a wife, my boy. I saw enough of that with my father. She cannot bear you children if you end up killing her."

Chase stared at him, and Enzo was struck anew at how amazingly innocent the boy seemed, despite his background. Innocent enough that he was still shocked by his close relationship to death in all its forms.

It was yet another reason to keep him safe.

He did not question his need to care for Chase. Something about the horror of Kirith and Laura's kidnapping, and Chase being included in the rescue, brought out his fiercely protective streak. He had to make all of that right once more. He did not feel the need to search too deeply for the cause of his feelings for Chase. They simply were, and that was that. Others found it odd, as his uncles surely did, their comments leading perilously close to angering him more than was wise.

A shout from outside took his attention, a loud thump against the side of the house making his eyebrow rise. Chase tensed beside him, still so afraid of conflict.

He frowned, rising to his feet. Chase should never be afraid, not here, not in his own home. He shot a warning glance at the boy, making sure he stayed where he was, out of harm's way, before he stalked to the double glass doors that led to the patio area and swung them open with anger barely shielded.

His gaze swung over the area, swiftly analyzing the situation.

The women were gathered to the right of the pool, several pressed close to a tiny Asian woman, who had tears in her eyes.

To the left, there were two groups embroiled in a scuffle. Most of the guests had moved back and away.

His livid gaze caught and lingered on one particular individual, his temper rising.

Of course, it would be Ilario. Who else?

He strode forward, his bare feet soundless on the stone.

Raymond stood in front of John Cho, holding him back, obviously trying to calm things down, while Enzo's ignorant pup of a cousin, Ilario, stood shouting insults, handsome features twisted in fury, a livid mark upon his cheek testament to an ugly encounter. Sergei was holding the young man back, and the disgust in his expression only reinforced his initial impression that this was all Ilario's fault.

"Silence!" His voice cracked over them. An instant uneasy quiet fell upon them as they watched his approach.

"I cannot step out for five minutes before disputes take place?" His gaze pinned his cousin before sliding to Cho.

The thirty-five-year-old, head of his operations in Asia, shook off the guards and straightened his suit, sending a rage-filled glare in Ilario's direction, before bowing his head slightly to Enzo. "I am sorry, my friend, but he has been harassing Jen despite everything she has done to discourage him, and then he pinned her up against the wall when she went inside to the washroom, tried to grope her." He snarled then, fists clenching. "So I fucking hit him, and now he acts like he should be safe from retribution. Because he is a Martinelli."

Enzo turned to face his cousin, feeling rage trickling through his control. He stalked forward, and Ilario's eyes widened a moment before he backhanded him. The young man stumbled to the side from the force, only Sergei's grip keeping him on his feet.

"*Idiota*! You dare to disrespect Joe's wife, here, at my home!

And then use our name to justify your actions! You earn that name, and so far, I have seen nothing, absolutely nothing, to tell me you are worthy of it. I have given you warnings before. No more. You get your carcass off of my property and don't return. I will tell your father of your actions, and he better give you a beating, or I will." He grabbed the twenty-year-old and hauled him up to meet him face to face. "If I come across you abusing our name again to cover your stupidity, I will personally end you. *Capisce*?"

Ilario nodded frantically, sweat trickling down his face.

Enzo tightened his fingers, part of him ready to punish the boy further, but gradually his madness faded to where he could feel the weight of eyes upon him. He could make an example of his cousin, here and now, renew the fear that others felt toward him…

Then he remembered Chase, probably watching, and his fury waned abruptly. He cast Ilario from him, back into Sergei's less-than-gentle grip.

"Get him out of here. He is no Martinelli I will acknowledge."

He watched Sergei drag the pale-faced young man away, before turning back to Joe, who now had Jen sheltered under his arm, the small woman clinging to him.

"I apologize, my friend. He is a fool, but never would I have thought he would be a suicidal one." He bent to Jen, taking her hand gently in his and kissing the back with courtly reverence. "I am so sorry that this happened here, to you. My guests are supposed to be safe. He will never be in your presence again. And if he should ever try to contact you in any form, I will see a final justice done."

Jen blushed, looking up at him through thick black lashes, her small face so perfect, rather like a delicate porcelain doll. "Thank you, Mr. Martinelli. I should have come to you earlier and this would never have happened, but I thought he might realize how foolish he was being."

Enzo curved his lips into a grim smile. "That one will never learn." He reached out to shake Joe's hand. "I owe you, Joe, for not killing him."

"And bring your uncles down on your head?" Joe snorted, his fingers closing around Enzo's for a firm shake, confirming their continued alliance. "I know all too well how they wait like sharks for their chance."

Enzo could only nod. His uncles, both of them, had criticized his leadership of the family since his father's death, but he was too strong for them to be blatant in their disapproval. It was words only, for the moment, though Enzo trusted them not at all. They wanted power, and they desired it so greatly that family loyalty was bound to collapse at some point. They were the ones who had demanded Kirith's execution after he had killed his father, Enzo's father. It was well they had backed down, accepted Kirith's exile instead, because he would not have hesitated to have them killed. If it came down to them, or his brother, there would be no contest of loyalty.

For now, they all played the part of close family, of unity and strength to display to the cutthroat world they lived in.

He watched his back.

That it had become common knowledge that there were divisions was never a good thing. Outsiders would love to see the Martinelli empire crumble. If they could kill him.

He smiled to himself. Live by the gun, die by the gun. He was surprised he had lived this long, but he was cautious, and without trust, and perhaps that had served him well. He considered things once more, deciding that perhaps it would be good if Stacey was moved elsewhere for her pregnancy. She could be protected, and his uncles did not need to know of his child. It would keep things calm for longer. Something, some long-honed instinct, told him that his uncles were growing impatient, that they were maneuvering in some fashion that would be dangerous for him. He kept spies on them, but they were true Martinellis, secretive and brutal.

And now this. Ilario almost deliberately acting out against a valuable ally.

He waved a hand, and Raymond appeared by his side, lips tight and thin. If Enzo had given the least signal, Raymond would have slid one of his ever-present daggers between Ilario's ribs without the least hesitation.

"He was deliberate about it, waiting until I was on the far side of the room, apparently." Raymond's smooth voice held distaste. "If you want..."

Enzo shook his head, laid a hand upon his assistant's tense shoulder. "Not yet. Perhaps in the future though, I might set you loose."

Raymond nodded, then drifted away from him, seeing to his duties.

Enzo spent time with the guests, seeing everything settled once more, soothing ruffled feathers and reassuring. When the relaxed atmosphere he desired for the party finally returned, he turned back to the house. A flicker of movement at the corner of his eye caught his attention and he turned his head, meeting Stacey's uncertain expression as she began to approach him. He stared at her silently for long moments, before pointedly ignoring her. She veered off to the left, wisely. Her earlier attitude still grated on his nerves.

Chase looked up as he entered, the young man's expression anxious, body held tensely. He laid a comforting hand on the boy's shoulder before seating himself once more.

Chase watched him for long moments, but soon returned to eating, his trust in Enzo obvious.

Enzo could not settle though, his mind far from this room.

It would be interesting to see how this played out. He could not wait to pit himself against his kin in blatant warfare. They had tried to harm his brother. So like his father, Enzo would not forgive or forget.

* * *

Daniel scowled as he spotted the school secretary hurrying his way, her face creased in lines of worry. The damned woman was always fussing about something, and she seemed to think that he cared what others thought. He'd have to set her straight soon enough, but for now…

"I'm so glad I caught you, Mr. Wayson. A parent has come to speak to you, and I—"

Daniel Wayson arched a haughty eyebrow. "A parent? Without contacting me first? I don't have time to see them. Tell them—"

The secretary grasped his arm and began to tow him behind her in a forceful manner unlike anything she had displayed before. "I'm not telling him anything, sir. If you want him to leave, you're going to have to tell him yourself. He's not going to leave on my say-so, and he's truly scary."

Daniel sighed, rolling his eyes. The pitiful little female obviously needed his strength of manner to rout this no doubt blustering parent. He frowned, wondering which student had complained. Normally they were all too cowed even to think of crossing him, but there were a few. He would have to put this parent in his place with all speed. Showing up without an appointment. Who in hell did this father think he was?

His outrage grew the more he thought of it. He was too important to be treated in this manner, and he could well see the student removed from class if his pride demanded it. They'd see how foolish it was to lock horns with Daniel Wayson.

He shook off the annoying grip on his arm as they reached his office, watching the secretary scurry off. Growling under his breath, he opened the door with some force, stalking into the room, ignoring the figure seated before his huge desk as he slammed down the books on its gleaming surface as a testament to his temper.

He took his time seating himself, then steepled his hands and peered over them, ready to put this intruder in his place.

Daniel froze.

There was not one man, but three.

The man seated before him looked more as if he'd stepped from the pages of a fashion magazine than any parent Daniel could remember, even though the children who attended the school were all wealthy. His suit was crisp and perfect, screaming money, his posture languid, and yet with something that was more predatory than relaxed.

The two men behind him, next to the door, stood in silence, hands clasped before them, eyes trained on nothing. Obviously bodyguards. Daniel's mind scrambled over his students, desperately trying to ascertain who on earth this man could be. His feeling of superiority was fading under the atmosphere that seemed to permeate the very air of his office.

The parent stared at him in potent silence, dark eyes half-lidded. There was no impatience in that look — nothing much at all to glean from it. It was eerily neutral, and yet Daniel sensed threat of a sort that made him swallow hard.

"So, Mr....you're here to talk about which student? Since you didn't make an appointment, I have nothing ready to discuss with you." He was proud of the steadiness of his tone, even though his hands, safely out of sight beneath the desk, were beginning to shake despite his best efforts.

The man raised an eyebrow in silent mockery, retaining his silence for a few more moments. When he did speak, it had been made very evident that he chose to, not because Daniel intimidated him in the least.

"My name is Enzo Martinelli."

Daniel's hands spasmed into fists, his eyes widening. That name was all too familiar in upper echelons, whispered more than spoken out loud. Daniel had heard every lurid tale, every bit of gossip that circled through his family and friends.

This was not a man to cross. Ever.

He realized the silence had gone on too long and cleared his throat, trying to control the tremor that wanted to take his voice.

"Mr. Martinelli, I'm honored to have you here." He reached across the desk with one hand, praying his fingers wouldn't tremble.

The Martinelli looked at his hand for long moments, then leaned back in his chair, loose and relaxed, but his eyes... He resembled a dragon viewing its prey with lazy interest all too much.

"I have come on behalf of my ward." The words held a bite to them, an indication of trouble. Pulling his hand back, Daniel wracked his brains, stunned. He had had no idea that the Martinelli even *had* a ward, much less that the ward had come to this school.

"I'm afraid I have no knowledge of which student..." Daniel hoped he had injected the right amount of dignified apology in his tone.

Dark eyes narrowed for a moment, then a faint smile tilted those generous lips.

"Chase Connors. He is in your English class."

Daniel froze, breath suspended for long moments. Dear God.

He struggled for composure, feeling danger slide into the room like a physical presence.

"Chase, yes. Talented boy."

"Your marks do not reflect that, Mr. Wayson. It seems from what I finally managed to get out of Chase, that you have an issue with him. Or perhaps more rightly, with his sexual orientation. I had thought such things to be quite illegal, Mr. Wayson. It seems I was wrong to assume such a thing is a deterrent to you."

Clammy sweat broke out on Daniel's forehead, and he had to wipe his palms on his pant legs. "No, certainly not, Mr. Martinelli. I just have found Chase's writing to be gradually becoming less—

cohesive. I have no choice but to…"

The Martinelli leaned forward, hands clasped together, eyes clear and cold.

"Do go on. But do so knowing that I have read each of Chase's essays. English may not be my first language, Mr. Wayson, but I know good writing when I read it. I have noticed no perceivable difference between what he wrote before you discovered his sexuality and afterward. It seems to me that the difference was you. Are you discriminating against my ward because of his gender preference?" The question was quiet, but the weight of it hung like a sword over Daniel's head.

"Certainly not, Mr. Martinelli." Daniel managed to inject just the right amount of outraged righteousness into his tone. "Chase has the same privileges of every other of my students. I can assure you—"

The Martinelli leaned further forward, and a trick of the light seemed to make his eyes gleam eerily in the stark lighting of Daniel's office. "No, Mr. Wayson, I can assure *you* that if I hear the faintest whisper of sexual bias regarding Chase, or for that matter any of your students, I will not hesitate to display to all and sundry your penchant for sadism clubs. I think that the prim and proper faculty you hold so dear would be most interested in your doings."

Daniel froze, his eyes fairly bugging from his head. He'd been so very careful, so very discreet. It wasn't possible for this man to know…

Enzo leaned back again, the faintest hint of a feral smile tugging the edge of his mouth. "I know a great deal about you, Daniel Wayson. Those who bring themselves to my attention often find themselves in—shall we say—difficult situations. Sometimes career-changing situations. Be thankful you have gone no further than you have. You would not like to know what happens to my enemies." The voice was so perfectly smooth, so utterly cold, that Daniel couldn't help but shiver, his eyes fixed upon this predator that had, within moments, turned his life on end. He couldn't speak, could not even rise politely to his feet when the Martinelli rose and bestowed a terrifyingly gentle smile upon him as he turned to go.

"You will be watched now, Daniel, at all times. I expect your behavior to be impeccable in all ways. If it is not…" Enzo shrugged. "We will have to have another—talk. I sincerely doubt it would be a pleasant time for you. I suggest you mend your ways, hmm?" That stare turned utterly cold, all signs of amusement disappearing.

Daniel could only nod, like a puppet, his body strangely numb, his thoughts fragmented and frantic.

"I am glad we understand each other. I hope I shall not have to encounter you or your sordid little life again." As if on cue, one bodyguard opened the door and the three men disappeared without another word.

Daniel leaned forward and buried his face in shaking hands.

Chase slammed his car door and practically ran into the house.

Sergei was closest to the door, and he instinctively reached for his gun at Chase's abrupt arrival.

"Where's Enzo?" Chase blurted.

The security chief relaxed into his usual expressionless calm.

"The boss is in his office."

Chase nodded and sprinted up the stairs.

For once, Raymond wasn't at his post in the outer office.

Chase paused at the double doors, uncertain for a moment. It was not wise to beard the dragon in his den, but… He could not help it. He raised his left hand and knocked lightly upon the ornate wood.

"*Sì?*" The tone held irritation. "What is it now, Sergei?"

"It's me, Enzo. Please can I talk to you for just a minute? I won't take long. I just can't wait…" He looked up in surprise as the door swung open and Enzo stood there, looking unbearably handsome in charcoal pants and a white button-down shirt with the sleeves rolled up to show muscled forearms. His face was blank for long moments, and Chase couldn't tell if he was annoyed or not, then he turned away and gestured him into the sanctum, one hand running through thick black hair with a certain amount of exasperation evident. Obviously things weren't going smoothly in whatever business he was currently dealing with.

"Could this not have waited until supper?" The growl in the tone made Chase shiver pleasurably, and he had to bite his lip to bring himself back to the moment—and the reason for his presence.

He waved the paper triumphantly before his mentor.

"I did it! I passed with damn honors. Can you believe that? Me—with honors." Disbelief lingered in his thoughts but he could not stop the stupid grin that seemed to have settled onto his features permanently.

Enzo turned, the annoyance passing away, his face softening ever so slightly, a smile tilting those generous lips.

"Honors? Congratulations, Chase! You have worked damn hard for this. You deserve every mark."

He laughed and twirled in a circle, uncaring of how childish he might look.

"Even Mr. Wayson changed his mind, seemed to mark me better these last two months and that brought my overall mark back up. Honors!" He twirled again and did a little happy dance that had Enzo laughing.

"Come here, my boy." He was swept into a hug. He almost froze, then slid his arms around Enzo's muscled torso, his smile fading. He wanted to weep for the force of the emotions he felt then, the touch of this beloved body, a gesture that was usually extended only to the Martinelli's brother and niece. He breathed deeply, inhaling every nuance of scent that he could. If only he had the right…

Enzo stepped back, releasing him, pride evident in his expression.

"You well deserve this. Now you are free to choose your college. I do not want you working, despite your pride. I want you to focus on your studies, *sì*?" He tousled Chase's hair with one hand, then put a hand on his shoulder, steering him toward the door. "I wish I could speak of this more, but I have a phone call coming in and I must take it. We will talk more *piu tardi*."

He nodded, smiled up at him in what he hoped was a normal manner, then exited the office, hearing the door close quietly behind him. He sagged against the wall, trying not to hyperventilate. *Oh God. He held me. I held him.* The smile returned but for a much different reason than the first time.

He pumped a fist in the air and danced down the hall, off to tell Ms. Granger and the guards of his honor standing.

Chapter Four

The Martinelli had abandoned the gloom of his office, and lay on one of the chaises, wearing only shorts, savoring the sun. Chase sat nearby, sensibly in the shade of an umbrella, drying himself off after swimming. He admired the lines of Enzo's body, the muscles evident even in relaxation. Such beautifully dark skin. He looked down at himself ruefully, at the pale skin that burned more than tanned. His body was lean to the point of being skinny despite the fact he ate like a horse. He just never managed to put on any weight, and his muscles were lean, not sculpted, like Enzo's. Scars littered his skin from his ordeal. It was hard to see anything attractive in himself against the backdrop of such raw, masculine beauty. He rubbed his wet hair, feeling his spirits sink. What chance did he possibly have ever to gain Enzo's attention? The man was surrounded by beautiful people—rich, accomplished, worldly people. What did he possibly have to offer?

He scrubbed his hair harshly, as though driving away his own thoughts.

He was enjoying his break from school, but found himself reluctant to turn his attention to choosing a college. The reason for that reluctance was all too obvious, even to himself. To leave Enzo…

So he lazed about, swam in the pool, tried to spend as much

time with his mentor as possible.

Enzo on the other hand, was in a foul mood, and people trod softly around him. Whatever the issue was, it continued for some time, and Chase did his best to act as an intermediary so that others did not bear the brunt of his temper.

Today seemed a little better. Hopefully the Martinelli's softer mood would last the day.

Their solitude was broken by the sound of brisk footsteps, and Chase looked up to see Sergei approaching, professional mask in place as usual. Honestly the man looked as though he might crack if he smiled. He shook his head at the thought.

"Sir." Sergei stood at Enzo's side, his head bowed slightly. "Ren Sylvesta is at the door, requesting your time."

Enzo raised his eyebrows sharply and opened his eyes, a hint of curiosity in their depths. It was obvious he knew who Sergei was referring to, though Chase had never heard the name before.

The Martinelli was silent for long moments, his gaze on Chase, before he nodded.

"Let him in. Bring him here."

Sergei nodded respectfully and turned away, leaving Chase staring after him in confusion.

His attention returned to Enzo, his silent question hanging between them.

Enzo waved a hand lazily. "An old friend. Have not seen him for…" He wrinkled his brow for a moment, a hint of surprise in the expression. "*Mamma mia*, could it be eight years already?" He shook his head in apparent shock, then rose to his feet, tousling Chase's hair affectionately as he passed.

Chase watched with a frown. Enzo claimed few as friends.

A man strolled through the double doors with an edge of familiarity — and Chase hated him on sight.

He was unbearably beautiful in an androgynous sort of way; face of an angel, wavy brunette hair that shone in the sun, green eyes that lit to fire the moment he saw Enzo. His body was lean and lithe, clothed in skintight black leather pants and a black button-down shirt that was open enough to show bronzed flesh.

"Enzo! Mi sei mancato amico!"

To Chase's increasing horror, Enzo held his arms open, and the other man walked into them, immediately giving the traditional kiss to each cheek — smiling, chatting softly in Italian — before rising on his toes to lick across the taller man's mouth, and then slanting his lips across Enzo's with hungry force.

His jaw dropped, and he clenched his hands slowly into fists. Who the hell was this guy? And what the fuck did he think he was doing?

Enzo did not seem adverse to the attentions. Indeed, he only smiled beneath the kiss, his arms wrapping around the smaller man, drawing him closer against his body.

He thought he just might faint. Enzo was kissing another man, and obviously not for the first time. But Enzo was straight, wasn't he? His heart seemed to want to pound through his chest, and he couldn't move for the shock of what he was seeing.

Enzo was bi.

Why the fuck had no one seen fit to tell him this rather important detail? He wanted to scream with frustration. If he had just known…

Enzo drew back from the kiss, one hand coming up to caress the other man's face lightly.

"Ren, *mio amore*, it is good to see you once more. It has been a long time." The softness on his face and in his words made Chase rise to his feet, shock turning to fury.

My love? What the fuck was going on?

Ren purred, damn well purred, as he pressed closer, his hands cradling Enzo's face, one leg rising to wrap around Enzo's hip. A sultry look from beneath half-lowered lashes. "*Ti voglio. Proprio ora?*"

Chase caught the gist of that, and by God… He cleared his throat, since Enzo seemed to have forgotten his presence in the firestorm this newcomer seemed to create.

The sound made the two men slowly part, though Ren gave a few thrusts of his hips before he removed his leg from its embrace. He turned his head, meeting Chase's angry stare with a raised eyebrow.

Enzo took a moment to respond, and Chase could clearly see the arousal tenting his shorts. The sight made him want to spit nails.

Who was this clown? How dare he act in such a way, in front of him as though he didn't exist! His anger grew with his thoughts. How dare he touch the Martinelli like that?

Enzo, to Chase's disgust, seemed pleased to see the newcomer, more than pleased if his cock was anything to go by.

"Ren, this is Chase, my ward."

Ren's expression grew calculating as he looked Chase up and down, as though he had suddenly become a rival when before he had been beneath notice.

He raised his chin, a feeling of determination rising in his chest. Whatever this man had been to Enzo in the past, he was damn well not going to waltz in here and screw things up.

The depth of the possessiveness he felt was rather overwhelming. The women who had slept with Enzo had brought a tight feeling and sadness, but this — man — was something else entirely.

The implications truly struck him and his gaze swiveled to Enzo, who was watching him with slight perplexity evident in his expression.

Did this mean Enzo actually slept with men? He was truly bi? This wasn't some anomaly? Chase wanted to groan with fury at himself. How had he missed this? He would have presented his feelings…

He cursed under his breath. No, he wouldn't have. His self-esteem was low as it was and his need of his mentor as friend, if nothing else, would have hampered him.

He hated this Ren already with his pretty boy looks and cursed self-confidence. He didn't deserve Enzo. He was the one who loved the Martinelli—not this interloper.

Ren gave a small smile and stepped forward, holding out his hand.

He stared at it with a black frown. A swift glance at Enzo showed his disapproval of the hesitation in manners. With grim reluctance, he returned the gesture, almost shuddering at the touch of that warm palm against his own.

"I did not know you had a ward, much less one so handsome." Ren's tone was playful as he looked over his shoulder at Enzo.

"You have not been present to know what is happening in my life, my friend." There was no chastisement in the tone. Enzo was obviously well used to Ren's absences. Chase could only hope that his stay would be short and his future absence even longer. His emotions must have been more evident than he thought, for Enzo was staring at him with a faint frown, and Ren was laughing silently, not seeming to be the least fazed by his attitude.

Chase wanted to punch his lights out, but he wouldn't lower himself to such extremes in front of his mentor. He was more than that, despite what burned within him. Enzo wouldn't appreciate a brawl in his own house.

Ren was evidently very comfortable here as he turned away and sank into one of the chairs with careless grace.

He looked up at Enzo with a seductive smile, holding out one slim hand. "I have been away too long. I missed your surly presence."

Enzo lifted a dark eyebrow, but his expression was anything but cold as he looked at the newcomer. Indeed, he crossed over and sank into the chair nearest to Ren, reaching out and taking that offered hand, his eyes glinting as he raised it to his lips, and bit one of the fingers playfully.

Ren yelped, then grinned, his own eyes lighting to fire in response to the sultry play. "Far, far too long," he whispered, leaning forward.

Chase cleared his throat again, having to grip the back of his chair just to prevent himself from stepping forward, the wish to come between them almost pulsing in his mind. The two men looked up blankly, as though they had forgotten his existence, as though they felt themselves to be alone.

He wanted to curse out loud.

Enzo met his furious gaze with his frown deepening, obviously unable to ascertain why his young charge displayed such anger in every line of his body.

Ren did not seem so confused. His half smirk seemed to indicate that he understood Chase's motives all too well. He reached out and gently caressed Enzo's cheek, encouraging the Martinelli to look back at him. "It seems your boy does not like to share. I suggest we go elsewhere, or if you wish, we could always go to the club…" His tone was pure seduction.

Enzo shook his head. "You expect me to wait? I do not think so, *mi amore*. Now." He stood and yanked Ren up to his feet, shackling his wrist in one powerful hand. He shot a glance toward Chase. "My apologies, Chase, but could you tell Ms. Granger that she will have to send food up to my room?" He did not wait for a reply, pulling Ren behind him as he strode for the double doors that led off of the patio.

Ren shot a look back over his shoulder at Chase, and his expression held nothing but triumph as they disappeared into the dim interior of the house.

He sank down bonelessly on the chair behind him, shock and anger battling for position in his thoughts.

Chase sat at the table, picking at the food morosely, trying to control the hurt he had no right to feel. Enzo wasn't his — and he had the right to take anyone he wanted as lover. But the shock had not abated that it was a man this time.

If Enzo was bi, that meant that he had a chance.

He shook his head, forcing the hope out of his mind. Enzo had always slept with those who knew the game. And not too young. Most were around Enzo's own age. Only Stacey was younger. Not once had his lovers been gentle or soft in nature as Chase knew himself to be. He could not see how that would be the slightest turn-on to a man who could have any desire at his fingertips. Perhaps Enzo saw him as less than whole, tainted by all those who had known his body? Why would the Martinelli settle for someone dulled with use, when he could have so many sensual offerings that had never known pain, didn't bear the scars of an abusive past?

If only…

Chase scowled to himself. He knew better than to dream. He had so much now, he should be grateful for everything Enzo had gifted him instead of wanting yet more.

He finally pushed the plate away, unable to face food at the moment. Ms. Granger came to the table, saying nothing, but laying a kiss upon his head. The sympathy and silent understanding was almost his undoing.

He dragged himself up to his room, flinging himself onto his bed and burying his face into his pillows to muffle his groan. He lay there for long moments, trying to get himself under control, then rolled over, leaning over the side of the bed to retrieve the stack of papers he had been gathering in the quest to choose a college. Immersing himself in the pamphlets, he tried to push aside the misery he felt.

Perhaps it was best he find a school far away, so he couldn't see what Enzo did each day, which lovers he chose.

Chase put a hand to his stomach, dismayed at the pain he felt over even considering a separation. How could he bear month upon month of not seeing the one he loved so much?

Peter, his therapist, had told him that the emotions would fade into friendship, that his feelings were not true love. Well, Peter, for once, had been wrong.

Seeing Enzo with another man had merely awakened the depth of what he felt. This was no mere gratitude or false lust. He felt this to the depths of his soul and knew now that it *was* love, to whatever degree he was capable of.

He rolled to his side and stared out his massive window, a tightness in his throat making it hard to swallow. The moon was almost full, and it lit up the patio and pool below with silvered brilliance. Movement sparked his interest, and he rose to his feet, switching out his light as he went.

It took moments for his eyes to adjust, and then his hand curled into a fist against the glass.

Enzo had Ren in his arms, the two of them standing nude in the shallow end of the pool, entwined. Ren had his face tilted up, and Enzo's fingers were buried in thick hair, holding Ren's head still as he ravished the smaller man's mouth with hungry fervor.

Chase caught his breath, leaning forward, longing for even a portion of what this stranger was receiving. Morality and self-preservation demanded that he step back, close his eyes as to what was happening below, but some part of him refused, denying even the pain to watch what he could never have.

He wished he could hear the sounds Enzo must be making, the mere thought of it making him shiver, his hand unconsciously sliding within his sweatpants to caress his cock, finding it already hard and weeping, so much did the scene affect him.

When Ren knelt in the shallows, looking up with a wicked smirk, before taking Enzo's cock in hand, Chase caught his breath, eyes fixed upon that beautiful member. Having been taken by so many, he counted himself a bit of an expert on male genitalia, and even from this distance, Enzo looked large and thick—and circumcised. He made a little sound in his throat, startling himself, his hand tightening upon his own cock.

Ren wasted no time, but guided Enzo to his mouth and commenced licking and kissing with evident enjoyment. He wished he could critique the performance, find fault with Ren's touch, but he had no right to criticize what the other man was doing out of clean desire. Chase had never experienced such a thing. Always sex had been painful—mentally and physically—and it had taken all this time for him to even want to touch himself, much less make love to another. But Enzo was different. The Martinelli was his touchstone, his safety. He knew he could lay with his mentor and come away with nothing but pleasure.

Envy crawled up his spine, making him grit his teeth. It was *his* right to hold Enzo, touch him so intimately, to explore that glorious body, not this—slut. He bit his lip, feeling shame cascade over his mind. How was Chase any better after what he had undergone? For all he knew, Ren loved Enzo as much as he did.

He shook his head in silence. No. Not possible. No one could love Enzo Martinelli as much as he did—to his very soul.

Below, the men stood in tableau, Enzo with head tilted back, lips slightly parted, legs far enough apart for Ren to handle him intimately without restrictions. His fingers were buried in Ren's hair, but gently, not forcefully, not yet. Chase watched the lean hips flex as passion rose, and felt his own cock fully harden as he handled it, beginning to flex his body in unconscious imitation of Enzo. He licked his lips, his breath starting to quicken as he watched the beauty of the men below. Their motions were those of lovers who had done this many times before, who were comfortable with each other's bodies; movements of grace, smoothness of purpose, knowledge.

Chase watched, and wished.

When Enzo cried out, he heard it even through the fogging

glass, and tears pricked his eyes as he hurtled toward his own conclusion. Panting, he watched as Enzo's hand slid down Ren's body to return the favor with his touch, but he could no longer continue as the voyeur. His orgasm had left him empty and cold within. He felt a million miles away from the men below and so very isolated in that moment.

Quietly, somberly, he went for a shower. He stood with his face in the spray, washing away the hot sting of tears.

College was beginning to look like an escape, rather than an exile.

Chase did not sleep that night and was early to breakfast — anything to get his mind off his troubles. Ms. Granger gave him a long hug, as though she felt his pain, and he had to fight back tears at her caring touch. Once she had disappeared back into the kitchen, he sat in silence, morosely rearranging his omelet so Ms. Granger would believe he had eaten something.

Footsteps from the courtyard made him look up, and a breath caught in his throat when Enzo strode into the room.

Enzo ruffled Chase's hair as he passed, and for once, Chase did not appreciate the gesture. It was something you did to a child, and at this moment, he wanted desperately to be so much more to his mentor.

"Your old bucket is leaking oil on the driveway again. Why will you not allow me to buy you a decent car? It is a mockery of my wealth to have that hulk in front of my villa." The teasing tone was familiar, as was the topic.

Today, Chase had no heart for such a thing. "I like my car," he merely stated quietly, his eyes lowering to his uneaten meal. After coming home with Enzo, he'd earned money at his first job — waiting tables at a restaurant Enzo owned — and scraped together enough to get his own vehicle. It represented independence, a new strength in him, in his life. He loved it dearly, rough though it was.

Ms. Granger bustled in, breaking the tension, and he could have kissed her in relief. He didn't know how to face Enzo this morning. The usual camaraderie and ease of their relationship was nowhere in his capabilities at the moment.

The only consolation was that there was no sign of Ren. He couldn't bring himself to question Enzo as to his whereabouts.

"You are very quiet, *ragazzo mio*. Are you all right?" Enzo's tone was light this morning, and why not? He had no doubt spent a very, very pleasant night with his lover.

Chase simply nodded, unable to meet those perceptive eyes.

He could feel the weight of his mentor's stare upon his face, so he forced a faint smile, though he still couldn't look up.

"I just didn't sleep well last night. Have a bit of a headache, so I will just take it easy this morning."

He placed long fingers under Chase's chin and lifted it so he had to meet Enzo eye to eye.

Enzo frowned, his stare deep and intent. When at last Chase found himself released, he felt relief of great proportions. Enzo was an expert at getting any and all information he wanted, whether that source be friend or foe. At least he was a little gentler with those he counted friends. He shivered. Never, ever, would he wish to be on the wrong side of the man he loved. The darkness that lived in those eyes was nothing that anyone would wish to face.

"You are avoiding the truth, Chase. What is going on?" The tone had dropped slightly, deeper, more commanding. He had never been able to resist that tone, for it was all too similar to old memories.

He bit his lip, dropping his head lower, feeling his body almost return to the curl his mind remembered so well.

A sigh. "Is this about Ren?"

He jerked his head up, his horrified eyes finally meeting Enzo's. He fidgeted, wanting to flee from the situation, but at the same time, feeling as though this was his only chance to make Enzo see, to drive Ren from the other man's thoughts and life. Something of his desperation must have shown on his face, because the other man leaned forward, true concern appearing on his face.

"Chase..."

Old insecurities were coming back to haunt him. What did he have to lose at that moment?

Silently he rose to his feet, and rounded the large table to stand before Enzo, close enough to touch. With every ounce of courage he possessed, he managed to meet those dark brown eyes.

Enzo turned his chair, frowning, obviously wanting to face him directly, and inadvertently providing Chase the opening he needed, wanted.

Before he could consider the consequences of such a maneuver, he caught Enzo's shoulders and dived in for a kiss, his fingers holding Enzo still.

Enzo froze, his lips parting in obvious astonishment, and Chase took the opportunity to sweep his tongue into that mouth, the taste everything he had ever dreamed of.

He closed his eyes, drawing in a shuddering breath, wishing the moment could draw out forever.

Enzo grasped his shoulders and pushed him ever so gently away, and Chase felt his heart shatter. With a gasp of pain, he whirled and fled.

He had destroyed everything.

Chapter Five

Facedown on his bed, he could not even cry. His chest felt so terribly tight, as if he would never be able to draw proper breath ever again, and his jaw hurt from clenching it so tightly in an effort to gain control.

Fool. He'd always known that he had to keep his stupid infatuation under wraps, but Ren's presence and the knowledge that Enzo was bi had opened something within him, something that demanded expression despite the dangers.

Now he would lose everything for a moment's bliss.

"Chase."

He froze, fingers clenching into the duvet, eyes wide and blindly staring at the wall.

His bed dipped beneath the weight of a heavy body.

"Chase, enough. Turn and face me." The command was light enough, but he obeyed anyway, though he couldn't tilt his face to meet those intense eyes.

"Chase, Peter spoke to you about what you were feeling. You know this is just growing pains, a need to love someone."

Something rose with him then, a rushing, pulsing rage he could never remember feeling before. He sat up, almost nose to nose with Enzo, grim determination driving him forward.

"Peter does *not* have a clue about this. Neither do you. I know what I feel, and it is *not* mere infatuation. Don't mock me!"

In some part of his mind, he was gibbering in horror at his words, at his actions, but something else drove him on. No one, not even Enzo, was going to get away with lessening what he felt. It was pure and clean and good, the best thing he had ever had in his life, and no one was going to destroy that.

The Martinelli was expressionless, nothing to glean as to his reactions to Chase's strange behaviors, both now and in the dining room.

"You have been greatly hurt in your life. I know you want someone. And you will find that someone, but it cannot be me."

He felt as though his very being were shattering into the tiniest of pieces.

"Why?" He hated the tremble in his voice. He wanted to be strong, to show his mentor that his feelings weren't a child's whim, but a true, adult passion.

Enzo reached out and gently traced his jaw with the lightest of touches, making him shiver.

"My boy, there are a multitude of reasons. Too many even to count."

"You think I'm filthy." He felt his voice crack, tears finally rising to his eyes.

Enzo shifted to grasp his shoulders and shake him slightly, enough that he had to look up and see the truth in his guardian's expression, the anger there.

"Never, Chase! I feel great admiration for your courage. Many could never have risen to the surface after such pain. You, you have done so much more. You are strong, brave and so intelligent. Never speak of yourself as anything less, do you understand me!"

He choked with shock, staring wide eyed at Enzo, speechless for long moments. At last he burst out, following the line of thought foremost in his mind.

"Why then? If you don't see me as tainted, then why? There are no reasons great enough…"

Enzo dropped his hands, ensuring no touch enjoined them.

"There are many reasons. And you need to understand them, so you can move on from this and find someone for *you*, someone with the purity of spirit that you possess. I cannot give you anything but support, my boy. My world…" He gave the faintest of smiles, the twist of his lips showing a hint of bitterness. "I am not for you, Chase. Everything about me is nothing that you should touch. It is bad enough that I have brought you into my home, making you a target, but I could not just leave you alone after what you had gone through. That is why I keep you separate from everything I do."

Chase stared at him. "I don't care," he finally whispered. "I don't care what you do or what you have done. I just want to be with you completely. Your friendship is everything to me, but my feelings are so much more. I cannot just deny that now, not when I have told you."

Enzo's eyes seemed a little sad, a little less hard for brief moments, before darkening back into implacability. "I am a killer, my boy. Coldhearted, brutal. I lead a life on the wrong side of the law, and my business brings harm to many. Many have died under my hand or by my orders. That is not someone to admire or to love. You need someone normal, someone who can give you a beautiful life."

"I just want you," he blurted, desperate. "I don't care about the rest."

Enzo shifted, and suddenly a blade lay on his throat, making him freeze in shock.

"Just weeks ago, I tortured a man, had my men kill him. I gloried in his blood, in his death." The shadows in Enzo's eyes flashed to full life, a certain madness glowing in the depths. "I kill, Chase. That is who I am."

He stayed steady against the blade, no fear evident in his

demeanor.

"No," he denied. "That's *not* who you are. That is what you were molded into by your father, your family. That's not what lies *here*." He laid a gentle hand over Enzo's heart. "I've heard the stories from Kirith. From a child, you were groomed to be the Martinelli, to kill, to lead killers. I don't believe that that is what you are. If you were what you think, you would never have taken me in. You wouldn't be capable of loving your brother, your niece. You wouldn't care for your people. You would thrive on the fear and pain of all those around you — not just your enemies — and you do neither. Please, Enzo." The name came with difficulty. "I need you, and you need me. Let me show you what life can be like when you are loved. Please…"

The Martinelli rose to his feet, the knife disappearing with an experienced flick. "You do not know what you speak of. You are almost half my age, and you have so much to experience. I would be the one to destroy you, and that I could not live with." The tone was final.

Chase rose from the bed, and approached with courage born of desperation. He reached up and cupped Enzo's cheek, letting all that he felt shine clearly through his expression.

"I'm not a child. I don't think I ever have been. You are the only one who has ever given a damn whether I lived or died or was ever worth more than a fuck. I have seen horrors, experienced them. I'm not a little innocent who doesn't know his mind. I may not be the strongest of souls, but I know what I feel and the depth of it. I love you," he breathed and wrapped an arm around Enzo's neck, drawing him down to meet his lips.

Enzo didn't resist, didn't respond, but Chase didn't give up, licking over those beautiful lips, giving the faintest of moans at the taste.

The sound seemed to break something in the other man's demeanor.

Enzo reached up, stroked back a lock of Chase's hair, and opened his lips.

"This is wrong, all wrong," he whispered, and Chase's grip tightened.

"No, it's right, perfect. Just give me this, please. I'm clean. You know that. I was tested after you rescued me and I have been with no one since. I only want you. I'll beg if you want."

Enzo shuddered, and Chase felt a thrill of victory sweep over him. "I'm yours. All yours. I want you so much. Show me what it's like to find pleasure. Show me what making love is like, instead of a fuck. Cleanse them from me."

Enzo raised his hands to Chase's shoulders and lay them there, flexing with his thoughts, his body tense, as though he prepared to push away.

"Please," he repeated, softly, pleading in his eyes, keeping them fixed on Enzo, willing him to accept, to…

"There is no such thing as love within me." Those lips left Chase's, and a coldness came over Enzo's features, the shadows clear and present within his eyes. "I am sorry, but I cannot give you what you need and want." He brought one long finger up to trace over his lips, then the Martinelli stepped back, turning away toward the door. He paused there, one hand on the doorframe, but not looking back to meet Chase's tear-filled eyes.

"*Fammi un favore*, Chase. I know this is difficult, but do not let this come between us. I—value your presence here and I do not wish…" He shook his head. "I cannot cleanse you. I can only hurt you far more than even Marcello managed. See me more clearly, and you will know there is nothing good that can come from this. Let us go on as we have."

There was silence as though he waited for an answer, but Chase was incapable of speaking, he could only clutch at his chest, at the pain that spiraled there in uncontrollable waves.

Enzo's fingers clenched for a moment on the frame, white-knuckled, the only visible response, before he stepped out, closing the door quietly in his wake.

Chase slid to the floor, a choking sob rising to his throat.

Chapter Six

Enzo leaned on the stone balustrade, drink in hand, brooding gaze fixed upon the manmade lake that lay below the vast villa, the moon reflected in its still waters. The view always calmed him, made the darkness that often drove him into restless and sleepless nights recede at least for a time. Tonight it held no serenity to ease his turbulent thoughts.

The breeze caressed over his naked form, a welcome relief after the heat of the day, but even that could not divert him.

He took a deep draught of the potent scotch, wishing it could dim his memories of the events that had transpired earlier.

Good God — Chase…the way he had almost begged. Telling Enzo he had not slept with another… That knowledge had almost driven Enzo to the edge. To know the boy was clean, as Enzo's latest test had shown he himself was, was a temptation almost more than he could bear. To be able to take him without any impediment between them…

He swore under his breath, trying to drive away the taste of that kiss. The boy had no idea of the potency of his emerging sexuality. He was healing — finally — and his libido was coming back into being. He was a healthy, beautiful, sexy young man who could have any number of admirers if he chose to open himself to the outside world. When he went to college…

The smash of glass echoed through the quiet night, and he blinked at the expensive liquor dripping down the wall from the force of his throw. The broken shards of his glass lay scattered over the balcony, glittering in the moonlight, and he glared at them for long moments, fighting the rage that rose within him. Violence rose like a specter, and he turned away from the night air, sweeping aside the curtains to his room.

Ren rose to one elbow, knuckling his eyes sleepily.

"Why are you still awake, *mio amore*?"

Those green eyes widened when they took in the predatory intent evident in every movement as Enzo stalked closer.

The rage rose higher. This was not who he wanted at this moment, but he would do.

He tried to shake off the rage. Ren was a friend, one of few and though he was always eager to absorb anything Enzo was willing to give, he should not hurt…

The anger spiraled higher, his thoughts becoming disjointed, vague.

He was distantly aware of flinging Ren over to his stomach and watching as his lover parted his thighs in invitation, back arching, a wanton moan making Enzo want him, now.

He fumbled for a condom, his breath shallow, almost panting with sudden powerful need. It rolled on and he positioned himself, brutal fingers sinking into the flesh of Ren's hips.

Enzo's sheathed cock speared him deeply and viciously, making Ren arch and scream, fingers clawing at the bed.

He sucked in breath and snarled in response, driving his hips into the heat that encased him. Ren met the fury, impaling himself on Enzo's cock with glorious abandon. Enzo did not speak, did not attempt to ensure Ren's comfort, he only set a hammering pace, deep and hard, that had Ren moving an arm in front of his head to protect himself, as he was driven against the massive headboard with relentless ferocity.

"Fuck, fuck, fuck." Ren's voice was ragged.

Enzo's breath began to echo in the room, coming in sharp, swift grunts, his anger a physical entity that encased them both.

He had never had a lover as intense as Ren, who could take what he dished out with such enthusiasm.

Would Chase… He groaned and thrust the thought away. Not now, he could not think of Chase that way, he could not.

Enzo gritted his teeth, clenching his eyes shut as the latest thrust actually lifted Ren's hips up and speared deeper than he had ever gone. So deep, so hot… He snarled, his thoughts once more spiraling away, his brutality rising.

Ren shouted a curse at an especially deep thrust.

"Yes, Jesus, harder — fuck it — oh yeah…" He drew in a gasping breath. "Ram me, baby! Show me you fucking own me!"

Enzo growled, a low ominous sound that made Ren shiver. He thrust harder, rotating his hips, the frenzy overcoming him, his body tightening, twisting, shuddering…

It seemed like forever, and yet only a moment before his orgasm came out of nowhere to slam him hard, breath freezing, body arched, feeling every inch of his cock as it continued to pound Ren's channel with relentless force.

It ended abruptly. Enzo gave a choked, haunted cry, his body pressed tightly to Ren's, fingers flexing upon already bruised flesh, his head thrown back for a long moment, as his body ruled his mind, driving away the darkness for a brief, precious time.

At last, he slumped over Ren. He felt Ren's body writhe beneath him, a choking gasp signaling Ren's orgasm. Then they stayed frozen in tableau, panting, exhausted. It took time for his cock to slip from Ren's channel, and for the smaller man to draw Enzo down gently upon sweat-wrinkled sheets.

"I am here for you, my friend. Always." He kissed Enzo's sweat-moist brow and drew him closer, a smile curling one side of his mouth, his eyes gleaming in the dim light.

Enzo searched for the peace, the comfort he had always felt in Ren's arms, but it was missing and he was all too afraid he knew why.

He let Ren stroke his body softly, but there was no after-release glow. No need for touch. He closed his eyes, the anger still simmering, but banked now, controllable once more.

Somehow, they would all get through this.

They had to.

He could not lose Chase.

The phone rang shrilly, persistently, and Kirith groaned, turning from Landon's warmth, to grope on the bedside table for the infernal thing that had roused him from deep sleep. His fumbling fingers finally located the device, and he managed the Herculean task of tapping the screen before pressing it to his ear.

"'Lo?" He was too tired even to inject anger into his tone.

"Kirith?" The soft whisper choked off, and a sniffle clearly could be heard.

Kirith frowned, trying to get his mind to function. "Chase?" He sat up against the headboard in an attempt to gain some sort of lucidity.

"I'm sorry I woke you. I just needed someone…" The voice broke off, and the pain in it jarred Kirith's senses. He and Chase had become very, very close during the time of Kirith's recovery, and even after the boy had left with Enzo, Kirith had made it a point to speak to him every time he phoned his brother. Chase had been doing so well — in school and in himself — so Kirith was shocked by this sudden breakdown.

"It's fine, Chase. I told you to phone anytime you needed me, and I meant *any* time, not just when it is convenient. You sound upset. What's happened?" He felt his protectiveness rise up. If anyone had hurt the young man…

"I did something so stupid." The whisper was choked with tears. "I should never have—I just love him, you know. He will hate me now. I have to go away…"

Kirith threw back the covers, shooting a glance at his lover as he did so. Landon slept on, like the dead. He shook his head fondly and then padded naked into the next room before shutting the door softly.

"OK, what is this about, Chase? Who are you…" He stopped, eyes widening with a sudden revelation. The few times Enzo and Chase had visited the island, Kirith had noticed something between them, but had dismissed it as a figment of his imagination. What if it was not?

"Tell me, Chase. I'm here for you—you know that—just as you were there for me before. There is nothing you cannot tell me." His voice stayed gentle.

"I kissed him. How stupid is that? He pushed me away, told me this is just a phase. It's not a phase, damn it; how could he even think that?" The voice of the younger man slid into fury and then back to despair.

Kirith sat back in his office chair, feeling the breeze of the open doors to the deck sigh over his bare skin, as he fought to understand Chase's words.

"You kissed Enzo?" Kirith could imagine the scene, and he flinched at the thought of his brother's reaction. He prayed that his brother had been gentle enough and realized how fragile Chase could be.

"I have to go away. Or something. I can't stay here. He is with that slut, and I can't watch them."

"Stacey?" Kirith questioned blankly.

"Ren." The tone held active dislike, and Kirith could well imagine why. He himself had never been fond of the man, though he couldn't put an exact finger on the reason. There was just something…off…about him. Kirith had been relieved when their affair had broken off and his brother had gone back to parading through a string of female lovers. So Ren was back. A coldness shivered its way down his spine. Something told him this was in no way a good thing.

Certainly not for Chase.

"Chase, calm down. Just tell me what happened."

"I...I could not take him being with a man. I didn't even know he was bi. I thought there was no hope. And then Ren came and I saw...things." A cry, quickly muffled, echoed through the phone. "I kissed him, and it was the most beautiful thing that I've ever done—and then he pushed me away. He told me that what I feel for him isn't real, that he isn't a good man to love. I don't care, Kirith. I love him anyway. I always will..."

Kirith rubbed his eyes. Personally, he could not think of a better person for Enzo than Chase, but he also knew his brother well. Enzo could be destructive to those around him, and Chase didn't deserve to be hurt.

"Do you want to come here? We would love to see you. Laura talks about you every day, and I know she would be excited to have you close again."

A shaky sigh from the other end. "Maybe. I would really like to see all of you, but I think, maybe, I just need to get my shit together and choose a college. I need to get out of here. I can't watch—I just can't. I love him." The sadness of the last words wrenched at Kirith's heart. If only his brother were capable of returning that love. They would be so good together, and Enzo deserved such devotion as Chase was able to give. Just as Chase deserved the protection and care of Enzo's softer side.

But reality made such a thing unlikely indeed.

The Martinelli lineage ensured that.

Enzo lived in violence, reveled in it at times when the darkness within him was at its peak. Chase was strong, but gentle in himself. Was he strong enough to endure the world that Enzo walked in?

"You need to think about this, Chase. You need to decide whether you are ready to endure Enzo's life. If he takes you, you will become a target more than you are right now. You will have to be able to stand up to him, show him who you are now. He still sees you as the fragile boy he rescued."

There was silence for long moments before a deep breath sounded over the phone. "How can I prove I'm more than that? He can have anyone he wants. What am I?"

"The one who loves him truly."

Kirith could almost see Chase chewing his lip as he often did when he was thinking deeply. "Stacey is pregnant with his child."

He damn near dropped the phone.

"What?" His voice must have been louder than he intended, for he heard Landon move in the next room moments before his naked lover flung the door open, hair on end, wild eyed, gun in hand. For long moments, Kirith almost forgot the chill of the news, so entranced was he by the enticing picture before him. Perhaps they needed to role-play more, because that pose was damned sexy.

He waved his lover down at last, shading his eyes with one hand so he could focus on the conversation. "Enzo did not tell me this!"

"He just told me the other day. He said that even if he married her that she wouldn't live with us, so...I guess that is something, right?" The tone begged for assurance.

Kirith pinched the bridge of his nose, sighing under his breath as he felt Landon behind him, strong hands kneading his shoulders in a comforting touch.

"Let me talk to him, Chase. I will phone him today — later — " he glanced at the clock with tired eyes. "I will find out what is going on with him. Perhaps..."

"You and I both know there is no hope, Kirith. Thank you for trying, but it won't do any good. Once Enzo has made up his mind, he doesn't change it. I just have to get on with my life. I had hoped that I could still have a part in his life." Chase's laugh was bitter. "But I can't watch this. It will always be someone else, not me. I have to find a path of my own, Kirith, create something that will keep me from being so foolishness." Kirith could hear the choked breathing for a moment, and he wished with all his heart that he could hold Chase, comfort him, as the boy had held him in the dark days after Kirith's rescue.

"Maybe, just maybe, I can get to a point where I can have his friendship again, be able to be in his presence without wishing for more." The tone held no particular hope.

Kirith cleared his throat, feeling his own emotions rise. How he wished, for Chase's sake, that Enzo would see the light, but he knew his brother too well.

Unless…

Thoughts coalescing, he sat up straighter. "Chase, there might be a last chance, something that would awaken any possessive feelings Enzo might have for you."

There was potent silence on the other end of the line, then Chase's doubting voice. "What could possibly…"

"Dark Whispers."

Landon stirred behind him, a hiss of surprise escaping his lips, before he leaned down over Kirith's shoulder.

"You would send the kid into *that* place? Seems a little risky to me."

He raised a hand to trace a finger over Landon's lips. "That's where you come in. Take him there, my love. Take a couple of the men with you. They'll love the break and you will all be there to see Chase is safe. But Enzo does not need to know that."

Landon straightened, and looked at him in disbelief. "Are you trying to get me fucking killed? Enzo hardly likes me at the best of times. If he sees me without you — there, with Chase — you think he won't gut me?"

"I will leave a message for Enzo, telling him I asked you to take

Chase out for the night. It's my brother's club after all. He owns the damn thing. Of course you would take him there, not knowing what it is. You have never been there."

"You are placing a lot of faith in Enzo taking the time to find a reason. He might just use the knife first, and question later. That frickin' knife is always on him. He's one scary fucker when he's riled, Kirith. I thought you loved me."

Kirith grinned and pulled Landon down for a deep kiss. "I do, completely."

"Then why endanger me and my balls like this?" Landon's tone was plaintive.

"You are fully able to protect yourself. Stop sounding like a helpless little virgin."

Landon grinned then. "Oh, no virgin here. Gave that to you, didn't I?" He bent forward to rake his teeth up Kirith's neck, making him shudder in reaction. It was all he could do to retain enough thought to remember Chase was on the other end of the line, and hearing everything.

Gently, he pushed his lover back, ignoring the growl of displeasure his move produced.

Chase's voice echoed from the phone. "I've heard of the club. Who hasn't? But, really, I don't understand what going there with Landon could possibly achieve."

"That is what we are going to find out. If it does nothing, then you know you might as well move on. If it does—be prepared. My brother's passions come from dark places. Be sure he is what you want, Chase, or you could be terrified of what he can be."

Chase did not speak for long moments, and Kirith was satisfied that the boy was considering things, not foolishly leaping into this.

"I want to try." Chase's tone started out softly, then morphed into determination. "If this is the last chance, I will take it. Thank you, Kirith. Thank Landon for me. I wish you could come."

"So do I." Kirith shook off the familiar longing for freedom.

"Someday. Enzo says he will make it happen. I can only wait for that."

Landon traced a finger down his face, and freedom faded from his thoughts. He had his lover and his daughter here, and that was all he needed in this world.

He sighed into the phone, eyes fixed on Landon. "Get ready, Chase. Hurricane Landon will arrive this weekend."

Chase found himself shifting from foot to foot, impatience thrumming through him as he waited by the front door. His behavior had finally attracted Sergei's attention, and he had had no option but to tell the security chief who was coming and where he was going. He feared that the grim Russian would immediately go to tell his boss, but the huge man had eyed him for long moments before returning to his office.

He was not sure what that meant, whether condemnation or support, but he was too nervous to really dwell on the matter.

Landon had phoned him from the airport and was on his way to take him shopping before they arrived at Dark Whispers that evening. Just the thought of entering such a place was making his stomach jump, not to mention spending time with Landon alone. The other man was not all that much older than Chase, but he exuded a type of cocky self-confidence that always made Chase feel dull and unworthy. He knew it was nothing Landon meant to do, and certainly he respected the other man totally, for loving Kirith so completely if nothing else. Watching the two of them grow together after the horror of Kirith's kidnapping had been a true joy, and sometimes he still got emotional just thinking of the love between the two men. It was what he himself wanted so desperately with Enzo, and the fact that it seemed impossible, he placed on his own shoulders.

He was not enough for the Martinelli. That much was perfectly obvious in all ways, and Enzo had been right to push him away. That much was clear in the light of day. Chase wished that Landon wasn't coming, that they weren't going to play through this farce.

Then he took a deep breath and stood straighter. He had to be strong. He had to make a life for himself beyond Enzo, make his mentor proud, and relieve him of the burden that he was beginning to be with his unwanted emotions. Going to a nightclub, meeting others, was a good introduction into a world beyond this place. With Landon at his back, he would be safe, and perhaps could hone his social skills in a way he had never before desired. Before there had only been Enzo. Now there must be something beyond that, and he had no wish to be lonely when he went away to college.

A friend. That was what he needed, and although he had no expectation of meeting such a person at a place like Dark Whispers, it was a start in his quest for independence.

More than that could not come of this night, not even with the greatest of wishing.

When the car carrying Landon finally arrived, he left the house, closing the door behind him with a sense of grim determination.

Chapter Seven

Enzo entered the house, sighing with weary relief. Raymond was right behind him, hard at his heels.

The assistant nodded to him, looking just as worn as Enzo himself, before disappearing to work on their notes.

The day, mirroring his mood, had been difficult, and it had taken all his reserves just to act like a rational human being, instead of taking out his inner fury on his subordinates. Something, somewhere, was going wrong in his dealings with the South American suppliers, and he needed to get to the bottom of it. All his senses were on alert. Someone was making a move, and he suspected his uncles, Benito and Paolo, although he could not rule out others outside the family.

Before, he would have relished the coming conflict. Now, he just felt annoyance and a certain degree of distaste, as though he wanted no part of what was to come. His usual eagerness to face dangerous challenges seemed strangely absent.

Loosening his tie with one hand, he nodded to Sergei, who stepped forward, drawing Enzo aside.

"Well?" Sergei as ever was short and blunt, welcome after a day of lies and smooth words.

"We are checking the southern lines, and John Cho is making sure there is no influence in the Asian connections. Someone is fucking with us and I want to know who." Enzo could not work up the energy even to snarl about it all.

Sergei nodded, then shooed him up the stairs.

"I will send up food and you better damn well eat."

Enzo waved a hand in acknowledgement before tackling the stairs with slow, heavy steps. He paused for a moment at the top of the stairs, almost turning back to ask about Chase, but pride made him clench his teeth and move on to his rooms. He would only make things worse by pressing the boy at this time. Give him room, and hopefully he would see the insanity of his wishes.

He could only hope that whatever the outcome, that their relationship would survive. The thought of losing Chase entirely made his stomach clench, and he could not quite decipher the reason why. Only a short time ago, Chase had not existed in his world. How then had he managed to become an important part of each day? He had been a duty to begin with, a sort of symbol for all that had gone wrong, all the pain and suffering that Kirith had endured. He could not have Kirith close enough to be able to help the way he wanted, so somehow, Chase had attracted all those protective instincts that rose within whenever his brother was threatened.

Those instincts still ruled, and he wanted the best for Chase. He wanted to give him everything and anything at all. It was good that the boy had a growing streak of independence, otherwise he would have been hopelessly spoiled, something he had not even done with his own niece, little Laura.

The enduring abuse that Chase had undergone and his subsequent years of therapy had produced a connection of sorts between them. He respected Chase's strength, his courage in fighting to overcome what was within himself. He had only ever seen such a thing in Kirith, and to find it also in this young man, so broken, had intrigued him, caught his attention in full.

And yet, for all that strength, Chase was gentle, again rather like Kirith, although his brother had more of a temper, and the ability to be a dangerous force. At first, he had thought the similarities to be why he had kept Chase beyond the time of therapy and healing. In his mind, it seemed rather like the boy was a younger brother, someone to care for. It had seemed no more than that.

But now, with Chase's protestations of love — he did not know what to think, what to do. This was outside his experiences, and all his power and money, his prestige and reputation, gave him no help in this.

He frowned as he entered his rooms and threw the silk tie carelessly on the back of a chair. Perhaps he should phone Kirith. His younger brother seemed a little more inclined to understand emotional nuances. He knew that he himself had little talent in this direction. He was making a perfect muddle of this whole thing, but he did not have a clue how to dissuade Chase from his advances other than to be honest.

Look how that had turned out.

He flinched at the memory of hearing Chase's heartfelt sobs from the other side of the door. Everything within him had screamed to return, take the boy in his arms, and soothe away the pain, but he could not.

None of this was right.

With all the underhanded, seamy, bloodthirsty things he dealt with, at least he could be honest to himself.

He had no illusions about himself, knew exactly what he was and what was within him. There was no way he wanted to smear Chase with the darkness he carried. The thought of tainting that gentle soul with his bloodstained hands made him feel slightly ill.

His enemies, should they discover exactly how strongly he felt for the boy, would use this to their advantage, just as they had used Kirith and Laura against him.

He could not allow that kind of weakness.

Surely, a man such as him was meant to be alone. Surely that decision had been taken out of his hands, long, long ago, the moment when his father had congratulated him on his first kill.

Weariness settled upon him, so deep it felt like his body would be crushed beneath its weight. He toed his shoes off with effort, then rose to his feet, shaking off the heaviness with a shrug of his shoulders. Methodically, he unbuttoned his shirt, pulling the tails out of his pants as he crossed the room. He poured himself a glass of scotch and stood before the large French doors that led to his balcony. Drawing a deep breath, he pushed them open and passed into the waning sunlight, the pastel beginnings of the sunset just appearing on the horizon.

He sank into his chair, his favorite spot in the entire house, with a faint moan of appreciation. Its thick cushions welcomed him, and he felt his nerves begin to settle. This was his refuge from the world outside, the barrier against his responsibilities.

Here he could just be Enzo, and not the Martinelli, not the strong killer that was expected of him.

He let out a pensive sigh, swirling the scotch absentmindedly. He would have to speak to Chase tonight. It could not be left as it was—but oh, how he wanted to avoid it. He had not the faintest idea what to say, how to ease them past this stage in the boy's life. He was not used to this indecisiveness within himself. He was known for his clear head, cool, calm precision in all he did.

He could not say he liked this new side of him. It seemed like weakness, and yet…

It all came back to Chase.

He laid his head back and watched the growing sunset with half lidded eyes.

Chase.

The knock on the door roused him from his reverie, and he felt irritation spike for a long moment, before he thrust the emotion away.

"Entrare!"

Sergei entered the room with the silent grace that was so much a part of the huge man. Suitable, as he had spent many years as an assassin for Enzo's father, though now that life was behind him, as he had been chosen as Enzo's head of security. In his own silent way, Sergei was the closest to a true, loyal friend he had, and the two men had often sat out on this balcony, sometimes speaking, sometimes not. Either way they were completely comfortable in each other's company.

Sergei stopped at the small bar and poured himself vodka — straight — before venturing out onto the balcony, taking his own accustomed chair.

"So, where is Ren?" There was a hint of dislike in the tone.

"He wanted to see a play in Miami. I could not go because of that meeting, so I sent him on the helicopter. He has friends there, so it is not like he will be lonely. He should be back in a few days."

Sergei nodded, relaxing back into the cushions.

They sat in silence for some time. Sergei finally ran a hand over his short, military-cut blond hair before turning slightly in his chair, letting one leg lounge over the arm as he faced Enzo.

His silent scrutiny made him smile ever so faintly.

His friend would wait forever if necessary, if he thought he needed to talk about something.

They both knew what the topic would be.

"Have you ever wished you had done things differently, lived your life differently?" He took a bracing gulp of the scotch, thinking how inane those words sounded out loud.

Sergei snorted softly. "Different? You, me, Raymond…we are what we are, my friend. Even if we had had different childhoods, I think we would have ended up on the wrong side of the law. We like power too much and dislike rules equally."

He nodded, staring blindly out at the ever shifting sunset.

"Still, I cannot help but wonder." He shook his head. Sergei was right. He was where he had always been meant to be, and to wish otherwise was pure foolishness.

"This is about Chase." Sergei's tone held no doubt. Enzo could not say he was surprised. It was Sergei's job to notice everything around the Martinelli, and there was no way he could not have known what had occurred.

He did not respond, not in denial, but in that he had no idea what to say. There was silence between them for long moments.

At last he shook himself free of his morose and counterproductive thoughts.

"The boy thinks he is in love with me." His tone held no mockery, but a certain sadness.

"He *is* in love with you, Enzo. Whatever you might think, the boy lives for you. What he feels is no small thing, no phase of his life he will get over."

He felt a frisson of irritation. Sergei was making more of this than needed to be. "Then it is first love, and—whether you think so or not—it is because of what he has undergone. I am safe to him. He needs that security more than anything else, so he looks to those he knows."

Sergei shook his head, and his annoyance grew as his friend's eyes glittered with humor, something he only ever displayed to Enzo himself.

"You are being deliberately blind, mostly because this is too complicated for your senses. Chase is no weakling. He might be healing, but don't doubt his ability to judge things around him. Don't lessen what he feels as anything less than the truth."

He glared at him for long moments. "You suggest I fuck the boy then? Ruin him? Let him believe I have anything to give him more than I have?" He snorted. "As you said earlier, I am what I am. I cannot change that. Chase needs to be free and have no part of our world. I am almost twice his age, have you forgotten that? Perhaps what he feels is more of a father complex."

"You need to give Chase more credit. He is not a child. He is a young man who has been greatly damaged. Out of all that, beyond what happened, he found someone to love, a reason to keep going. Strong though he is, he would not have made it but for you. He looked to you, saw that you believed in him, and he clung to that like a lifeline."

He scowled. "He did it himself. I just gave him the foundation to step off of."

"He might have done it himself, true, but he did it *for* you, because of you. You gave him something to reach for, and that something was your acceptance of him, your pride in his achievements. Before you, he had no reason to try. He did not respect nor love himself, so he respected and loved you enough to do what he did."

He could find no answer, so he set his jaw and was prudently silent.

"You should take him to your bed, love him, keep him, and be fucking grateful you found him. Most of us would give our right arms to be loved like that."

He turned his head, staring at his friend in utter disbelief. "Have you heard nothing I have said?"

"I heard, and I am glad you see the difficulties, but if you do not do something, you will lose him, and you will regret it all your life." Sergei's tone held no doubt. "Chase is not going to be safe wherever he goes, so if you think staying away from him is going to help, think again, my friend. Everyone knows what he is to you, and whether or not he is your lover, he is in danger. As head of your security, I can say it would be far easier to protect the two of you together, rather than have you apart."

He blinked, speechless. Sergei eyed him, and burst out laughing.

He looked away, gritting his teeth, swirling the scotch in the glass with swift, irritated motions.

"I certainly hope you are not talking me into this for no better reason than that." His face smoothed, the irritation fleeing, a faint grin lifting the corner of his mouth.

"You make my job bloody difficult at the best of times. Anything I can do to make it easier…" Sergei had settled into a chuckle. "So—have I done it?"

He eyed him. "Done what?"

"Talked you into it."

"I still don't think you are seeing all the reasons that this is a very, very bad idea."

"No, I am balancing out your morose pessimism. You have to see both sides. But you better hurry, or you are going to lose out."

He raised an eyebrow, wondering what exactly his security chief was up to. There were too many nuances in his voice to ignore.

"Well, Kirith sent Landon to cheer Chase up, so he took him out."

He turned slightly, frowning at Sergei. "Landon left Kirith alone? What is that little…"

"He would do anything for Kirith, you know that. As I said before, Kirith *sent* Landon to take Chase out. No doubt Chase phoned Kirith, like he always does. He was a little upset after the run in with you, as you well know."

He felt a growl rising in his chest. "I am perfectly capable of looking after Chase. Why would Kirith do this, and not even tell me?"

"Actually Kirith phoned earlier, but you were in the meeting, and Raymond was with you."

The frown upon his brow grew larger. "I will have to phone him back and find out what the hell this is about. But more than that, where did Landon take Chase?"

Sergei tilted his lips into the faintest of grins. "Dark Whispers."

Chase found the club utterly overwhelming. If he had not had Landon at his side, and three of Kirith's men at his back, he would have turned tail and returned home, but Landon was giving him no options. He had him by the arm, a broad grin flaring to life as he viewed the dance floor, filled with writhing, gleaming bodies.

"Always wanted to try this out. Kirith and I dance at home, but this is something else. You and me, kid. Let's do it."

He squawked as he was dragged out into the mass of people. He stumbled and grabbed Landon, his fingers clenching in the new black silk shirt his co-conspirator wore. He could feel the hard muscle evident underneath, and he flushed, snatching his hand away as soon as he gained his balance.

Landon laughed at his blush, grabbing a hold of him and turning him around so his ass was pressed into Landon's groin, and they stood front to back.

He froze.

"Relax," Landon whispered, making him shiver. "Listen to the music, and start moving. Feel your body."

How the hell he could move plastered to that lean body? He fumed and tried to pull away, only to hear Landon chuckle.

"Just imagine I am Enzo. That should get this little ass moving."

He growled, fingers tugging at the grip Landon had on his hips, to no avail.

He huffed, already knowing that Kirith's lover was a whole lot wicked, certainly more so since he had been corrupted by Kirith himself.

He knew how to move, damn it!

Landon began to sway his hips, forcing him to keep time. He could not help but feel the press of Landon's groin, and his flush grew hotter. That particular package was all Kirith's, and he wanted no part of this. Really.

That smoky dark laugh swirled by his ear, and he shivered. Landon was all sexuality unleashed, a perfect partner for Kirith.

"Come on, kid. Show me what you got." There was faint taunting in the tone, and it got his blood up.

He decided to go with what Landon had suggested. Imagine this was Enzo.

It was hard to imagine Enzo lowering himself to stand with the masses to dance, but he could fantasize.

He threw his head back against Landon's shoulder and let go of his inhibitions. He imagined that he and Enzo were alone, those hands on his hips creating a link, a bond between them. He danced his passion, his need and the promise of what he wanted to give to the man he loved.

The hands remained firm, keeping him grounded enough not to lose himself totally, but the club faded away, and in his mind there was only he and Enzo, together, alone. Dancing as he had seen Kirith and Landon dance, all sexual innuendo and fire. Foreplay.

"Well, well, well. Seems our little ploy has worked after all. Damn, kid. He must feel something for you."

His eyes snapped open, and he had to center himself from his dreams, the harsh reality almost painful as it pressed in upon him. For long moments he had had what he truly wanted, and now it was cold as he came back to himself. Alone.

He blinked and then froze in place.

Across the floor, in the segregated VIP section, a tall, dark figure stood, arms folded over his chest, eyes fixed upon Chase.

Enzo.

He could only meet that disapproving glare, feeling himself begin to shrink into his grief once more.

Landon whirled him round and pushed deeper into the dancers. "Are you gonna let him do that? Just gonna bow down to him? He didn't want what you offered. Maybe you have to show him something different, hmm? Shake your ass, kid. Show him what he is missing." He could see the gleam of teeth in the flashing lights. "You want Enzo. You have to show him you can stand up to him. That guy only reacts to challenges, believe me. So challenge him."

He hesitated. The wildness that was so a part of Landon was nothing that he had ever found in himself, but—if it made Enzo look at him with even a faint hint of interest, it would so be worth it. *Last chance*, his mind whispered. *What do you have to lose?*

He looked up and met Landon's manic grin. He curled his own lips upward and nodded.

Landon laughed with obvious delight, and the dancers around them turned to look at the seductive sound. Many were looking at *him*, not just sexy Landon. He held his own attraction, his own allure. "Fuck," he whispered, in disbelief.

Landon stepped back and began to move, wicked eyes fixed on his, challenge in every line of him.

He grinned and began to imitate him, their mirror image drawing attention from several watchers. Landon grew ever more outrageous, to the point of lewd, and he followed, beginning to laugh at Landon's antics. He pulled his phone from his pocket, and set it to record his partner's sexy moves. "For Kirith," he mouthed, and Landon nodded, eyes growing hazy with desire at the mere mention of his partner.

He forgot his own dancing in lieu of carefully recording Landon for several minutes, catching the sexual essence of the other man in detail. Landon pulled his shirt free and dipped his fingers just within his pants, head back as he moved without the slightest hint of self-consciousness.

He felt his own heat rise just watching the performance.

If he could move like that, act like that, would Enzo see him as more than a fragile, damaged child? He was more than his past, he had at least learned that, but to shed it for even a few moments—

that was going to take some courage.

He put his phone away, shooting a glance over his shoulder. He could not see Enzo now; the press of bodies blocked all view in that direction, but he could feel his presence like a flame licking along his nerve endings.

He sucked in a deep breath. He wanted Enzo. He would do anything to have him, anything at all, and if that included reaching inside himself to bring out his latent sexuality, then that was exactly what he would do.

Flinging his head back, he began his own dance, no longer imitating Landon. This was coming from within, an expression of self that he had never experienced before. None of the people around him knew who he was. They could not pity him for his past or reject him because of it. Here, he was free of all that, and it was a feeling of giddiness that enveloped him then.

This time, he didn't dance for Enzo, he danced for himself, for all he felt within, and it was amazingly cathartic.

He didn't know how much time passed before he came back to reality, only that his body was sweat soaked and trembling, his mind calm and focused. He shot a look at Landon, who looked none the worse for wear, still apparently full of energy. He shook his head, grinning a little. Kirith had his hands full with that one.

And he was going to have his hands full with Enzo.

Because have him, he would. Some part of him held no doubt at all, and it was that part that made him move away through the crowd, determined to find the Martinelli.

When he reached the edge of the dance floor, he paused, searching the area he had seen Enzo earlier.

There was no sign of him now, and his stomach dropped. Surely he would not have left…

He prowled further along the edge, dodging people, then froze in place, eyes narrowing, hands slowly folding into fists.

Enzo was there, to the right of the bar in the VIP section. Who could be more VIP than the owner, right?

People were grouped round him, most at a bit of a distance, no doubt kept at bay by Sergei's scowling demeanor, not to mention the other bodyguards ranged silently some distance back, but others, perhaps employees, were close, their smiles fatuous, eyes gleaming with both avarice and admiration.

And one young man was…entirely *too* close. Slim, blond hair perfectly styled, clothes that did little to hide his body. Too damn perfect.

Seated beside Enzo on the lush cushions of the booth, he was leaning in, gently stroking Enzo's arm with a long-fingered hand, eyes hungry upon Enzo's face. The Martinelli was not paying a particular amount of attention. He had taken off his suit jacket and rolled back his sleeves, looking relaxed and completely at home in this place of debauchery, drink in hand as he viewed the boy with a certain amount of amused tolerance.

Two of the bodyguards stood near the sides of the booth, cold eyes watching every nuance of the crowd, while Sergei sat to Enzo's right, his presence more of a deterrent than six other men.

He gritted his teeth, feeling fury rise within him, as the boy traced his fingers ever downward, finally stroking over a tanned forearm.

This was too much. Someone else touching Enzo's very skin was the last straw.

He strode forward, almost pushing people out of his way, eyes fixed unerringly upon his target. The bodyguards recognized him, their eyebrows raising somewhat at his demeanor, but obviously seeing no threat in him, allowing him past. People watched in disbelief as he made his way through their ranks and entered the forbidden zone.

Sergei looked up, and he swore he saw amusement in the security chief's eyes, before they lowered to his glass.

Enzo took a deep swallow of his drink, then froze in place as he saw him approaching.

His dark eyes narrowed ever so slightly, then his expression smoothed into blankness.

He was not to be deterred. He didn't hesitate as he reached down and grabbed the boy's arm, hauling him unceremoniously off the seat, and letting him drop to the floor. The victim squawked in outrage, trying to scramble up, only to pause as he saw the fury in Chase's eyes.

Having vanquished the foe, he turned to the real challenge. Trying not to think of possible repercussions, he slid into the booth on his knees, maneuvering himself so he pushed the table back enough so he could straddle Enzo's lap, facing him.

The Martinelli froze, eyes wide, more shocked than he had ever seen him.

The sound of Sergei's laughter rang in his ears, as he slid his fingers into thick, black hair, holding it firmly as he slanted his face down over Enzo's. He felt large hands settle on his hips, no doubt to push him away, but he licked over Enzo's lips, moaning at even this small taste of heaven.

Enzo parted his lips beneath his as if he were going to speak, but he took charge, darting in his tongue to sweep over every surface he could reach.

So good…so hot. A groan rose in his chest, need rising, his cock hardening against Enzo's crotch.

Please, he begged silently. Just let yourself go; feel what I can give you.

To his relief, he felt a response, the cock beneath his beginning to stir. Enzo was being affected whether he wanted this or not. He flexed his hips, rubbing, deepening his kiss with all of the passion he had held suppressed for so long. The hands on his hips twitched, and he smiled into the kiss. Those hands were not pushing him away, not displaying the strength Enzo possessed.

The thought buoyed him, and he drove his tongue into Enzo's

mouth, inviting that other tongue to come out and play. The thought of others watching this byplay brought no shyness. Instead it made the heat rise higher. He wanted the world to watch. Enzo was his, whether he realized it or not. Of course, if Enzo reacted badly, his humiliation was going to be public knowledge, but this was his final chance. Perhaps the weight of watchers would still Enzo's possibly adverse reaction. Did he care enough about his feelings enough actually to protect him from being disgraced by rejection?

He was willing to exploit that advantage shamelessly.

The taste of that mouth… He whimpered, flexing his hips, feeling Enzo's cock hardening, the bar of flesh pressing against his own, rubbing deliciously. The thought of touching, stroking, tasting that intimate part of Enzo's body made him shiver, moving his hands down over the muscular arms restlessly, tracing the muscles through the dark blue designer shirt. The feel of that hard-toned body made him long to rip aside the barriers they both wore, to press naked skin against skin. Much as he wanted such a thing, he refused to unbutton Enzo's shirt. There was no way he was exposing his man to watching eyes. Enzo was not known for flaunting himself in public, and he instinctively knew that such a move would provoke a negative reaction.

He felt Enzo twine his tongue with his — a response at last — and felt hips thrusting ever so slightly beneath him.

He whimpered into the kiss. The feel of Enzo actually reacting drove his need higher. His whole body shuddered, as he felt Enzo growl under the assault, the fingers on his hips tightening painfully for long moments. He lifted his gaze and met dark, smoldering eyes, something rising within them that should have made him fearful. A hint of the shadows that made the Martinelli so dangerous. But he met the look with one of his own. Full of need and want. Pleading. He did not flinch from the proximity of those shadows. They were part of the man he loved, and he had seen far too much darkness in his life to step aside from this. He would show Enzo what was beyond the shadows, a place the Martinelli had never ventured.

He knew, in his very being, that he was the only one who could do this. It gave him strength, gave him a deeper determination than he had ever known.

He may want Enzo, need him, but the Martinelli needed him just as much. He just did not understand that yet. It was up to him to show the crime lord what lay beyond the world that he ruled over.

There was so much more.

Taking a deep, shuddering breath, he drew back a little, licking his lips at the taste of Enzo that lingered upon his mouth.

Enzo blinked, his intensity fading somewhat as though he realized where they were and what was truly happening. He did not give him time to think, to allow that iron will to come to the fore.

He stroked one hand over a lean cheek, glorying in the touch. "I want you to take me, to show me what it is like to have true pleasure. If you don't, I will have to find another…" He let the words trail off, watching the rage flare in those fierce eyes. "I need to know, I need to experience something other than pain and humiliation. I trust you, and I love you. Please, don't make me go to someone who has no care. I need this—I want this so much." His whisper feathered over Enzo's skin. It was risky, appealing to Enzo's possessive side, but it was all he could think of. The look that Enzo had worn when he had been watching him dance with Landon had given him hope. Now, with bated breath, he played his last card.

Long fingers came up to wrap around his wrist, halting his touch, and he felt his heart sink.

A long, low growl rumbled from Enzo's chest, and the fire in his eyes darkened still further. "Get up," he ordered, the tone soft and yet dangerous.

He wanted to weep with the sense of failure that overwhelmed him then.

Sliding from Enzo's lap, he scrambled to the edge of the booth, trying to control his expression, feeling Enzo moving out behind him. He could not look up, could not meet those dark eyes.

He could not draw a true breath. His chest felt tight and painful.

He heard Enzo bark something at the bodyguards, at Sergei, then fingers shackled his wrist, pulling him along behind Enzo's tall, intimidating figure. The Martinelli strode through the ranks of people, his mere presence seeming to create a path through the onlookers of the crowd, who watched him with wide eyes.

The rush of fresher air outside stung his lungs as he hurried in Enzo's wake, grimacing at the tight grip that ground his bones together. His mentor was truly angry, and he had no one but himself to blame for being on the end of that fury. His behavior had been utterly inexcusable. Now he would pay the price.

He blinked back tears as he saw one of Enzo's Jaguars pull up in front of them. Enzo yanked open the back door before the driver could even get round to open it for him and pushed him into the vehicle before following, slamming the door in his wake.

Chase pulled himself upright, cringing against the far door, rubbing his wrist slowly, wondering how much worse he had made things with his foolishness.

He felt Enzo move closer, then he was pinned against the door, Enzo's mouth crashing down on his.

Chase let out a startled cry that was muffled by Enzo's lips, disbelief keeping him motionless for long moments, then he let out a moan of need and responded with all the love he had kept bottled up for so long. He slid his arms around broad shoulders, and he gave himself utterly, completely pliant to whatever Enzo wished.

His submission provoked a rumble of pleasure from the older

man, and he yelped as Enzo wrapped a powerful hand around his leg and yanked him across the seat, so that he lay on his back under Enzo's body. The feeling of domination made him pant, whimpers echoing under Enzo's kiss. Chase slid his fingers down powerful arms and then caressed over hard pectorals as he blindly fumbled for the buttons of the silky shirt. Skin, he needed skin. He had to touch, had to… Please, this couldn't stop. He would die if this ended now. Just once, just…

Enzo ended the kiss, trailing his lips down over his neck, nipping, leaving reddened marks upon tender skin.

He reveled in the feeling of being possessed, of being wanted. This was so much more than he had ever received. He arched as much as he could under Enzo's weight, pressing against the hard arousal he could feel against his own. He managed to unfasten several buttons with his shaking fingers before plunging his hand into the space provided, closing his eyes as he touched hot skin. He traced downward, his cock jumping as he felt a taut nipple rub over his palm.

Enzo shuddered, the first sign that he was not completely in control, and a growl escaped his lips as he returned the favor, contorting on the seat as he shoved Chase's shirt up, and captured one of his nipples with his teeth, beginning to lash the captured flesh with his tongue.

His head arched back into the leather upholstery, staring with wide unseeing eyes at the roof of the car, a muffled scream locked in his throat. The sensations of pleasure and pain were all he had dreamed of, all he had imagined in the long lonely nights when he had wished for exactly this moment.

That this was happening was almost more than he could comprehend, but if this were a dream, he prayed that God would never let him wake. He would happily remain here for eternity.

He cursed as Enzo nipped hard, marking him, before moaning as he realized that Enzo had cleverly unzipped his fly, his now bare cock rubbing against Enzo's pants with delicious friction.

Enzo twisted, unzipping his pants, pulling his cock free. Chase licked his lips, rising then to push Enzo back so he was sitting on the seat, bending over him. Without pausing, he swallowed that beautiful shaft, feeling Enzo shiver, a large hand stroking over his head, sinking into his hair to hold him close.

For once, he felt no shame of his sexual experience and skills. For this moment he blessed them, that he could give Enzo pleasure, confidence in every stroke of his tongue, in the relaxing of his throat as he took the thickness deep, before turning his attention to the broad dark head, lapping at its slit, moaning at the taste. He pursed his lips, sucking gently upon the head, drawing forth that slick moisture that tasted so amazing upon his tongue. Taking Enzo's essence into his own body.

Enzo groaned, hips flexing, head flung back. Chase twisted his head just slightly, watching avidly, memorizing every expression of pleasure that flashed over the Martinelli's face. He was so damned beautiful. When he finally looked down, those dark eyes flared into something dangerous, something primal and deep that knew no boundaries.

"Get those damned pants off," the growl had him lifting his head, giving a last loving lick to the crown as he squirmed to remove the pants in the confines of the back seat. He glanced outside at the traffic, feeling heat rise in his cheeks, but also a kind of wild thrill at the exposure. The windows were tinted, but not that dark. More likely, it was the driver who was seeing this all quite clearly. All he could think of was pleasing Enzo, and the rest of the world hardly mattered.

Enzo pushed a finger within his mouth, and he sucked eagerly, never taking his eyes from his lover's face.

The Martinelli watched his mouth, his breath becoming harsher, his other hand tracing his lips.

"Such a beautiful mouth," he whispered, the sound harsh with want and need. "You looked good with my cock between your lips, stretched wide around my girth. I could come just from watching that, but I want to be in you, deep in your body. You better be ready, Chase, because you have wakened the dragon, and I am not going to stop, even if I hurt you. I tried to warn you."

He released the finger, wet and hot, spreading his legs wide, and leaning forward to meet Enzo's lips. "I want you. I am meant for you, and I will take whatever you give me with joy. Show me. Take me. I will not break, and I will not back away from you. Ever."

Enzo snarled, lips curling, yanking him closer, as his wet finger pressed insistently upon his entrance, sliding in without too much resistance.

Chase gasped, breaking the kiss as he tilted his head back. His hips pressed back, desperately seeking more. When the finger pulled away, he left out a soft cry of protest, watching with half-lidded eyes as Enzo smeared two fingers through his own pre-cum, coating them liberally before reaching between his thighs once more.

A mewl escaped Chase's throat as he was pierced, rising further up on his knees, his hands gripping Enzo's shoulders through the soft shirt. His fingers kneaded restlessly over the hard muscles as he focused on the sensations within him, as those fingers scissored and thrust, opening his channel that fluttered around the beloved touch. He shook with need, eyes wide with wonder over how different this felt than what had gone before. The men who had used him without care—who had beaten him, raped him, seen him as less than human—had never touched him so gently, and it was as though Enzo's touch was healing him from within…as though he were overlaying everything that had gone before with something so much greater.

He felt tears spill down his cheeks, and the movement of the fingers stopped for long moments, until he lowered his gaze to

Enzo's piercing stare. Those eyes searched his, then the inner touches resumed, harder and deeper. He writhed on the impalement, soft gasps escaping, eyes locked upon that fierce face.

With no more preparation, Enzo guided Chase over his rampant erection. He reached for it, positioned it, sinking down upon the length before Enzo could even thrust upward.

The burn was harsh and tearing, and he gritted his teeth, jaw clenching. Even this was good. This time there would be pleasure, a loving touch that came after. So different, so beautiful.

Enzo maneuvered him into place, hands settling on his hips, holding him firmly as he lifted him, then thrust up even as Chase sank down once more. He gave a short scream, pain and pleasure intermingled, as the Martinelli began to pump into him with harder, longer strokes that hammered his prostate with precise torment.

Everything faded away. The past, the present, what was to come. There was only this moment, the feel of Enzo beneath his fingertips, the thickness of his cock within his body, the heat and sweat and sheer pleasure of it all. His own cries overlaid with Enzo's growls and harsh, ragged breathing. Each stroke seemed to lift him higher, and he began to shake uncontrollably, the sensations rising to a plateau he had never encountered before. He had been right. He was meant for Enzo, even as the other man was meant for him. Nobody would ever give him this much. Nobody else. Only his Enzo.

The muscles of his thighs cramped, his body tightening to where it was hard to breathe, hard to...

His breath exhaled in a keening wail as he exploded, his body arching until his shoulders lay against the back of the passenger seat, his head tilted so he never lost sight of his lover's face. He had to watch, had to see...

Enzo's eyes were fixed upon him in return, and the fire, the darkness within, rose and twined together, before he thrust a final

OUT OF THE DARKNESS 99

time, deep and with such force that Chase was lifted up, impaled utterly, suspended for a long moment. The Martinelli gave a groan that rose into a roar, his body shaking as he came, fingers spasming on Chase's hips, bruising him with the force.

There was no sound then but their panting breaths, the noise of traffic around them. He felt hands grip his waist, slide around his back, pulling him forward so that he draped over Enzo's body, his head laying over his shoulder against the top of the back seat. He could feel Enzo's hot breath against his shoulder, feel the tension that flowed out of the other man to leave him lax against the upholstery.

Enzo hummed and laid him down upon the seat, looming over him for a deep kiss.

Chase lifted a trembling hand to comb through the rumpled dark hair, searching Enzo's eyes with wistful intensity. Had it meant anything to the Martinelli at all, or had it just been that he had driven him to that need, that want? A simple matter of sex.

The darkness that dwelt within Enzo did not show in his eyes at this moment, there was a hint of confusion, a scrap of softness that Chase had never seen before, except with his small family.

Enzo bent and laid his lips over his, and Chase flowed into the kiss with all his soul.

Whatever would come after this, he would hold Enzo's touch in his heart. This had been a gift beyond price.

Chapter Eight

Enzo stepped from the helicopter, bent low as his enforcers ushered him to the waiting car. Free of the overhead blades at last, he straightened, nodding to the man who held the car door open. He slipped into the back seat, Sergei and Raymond close behind him.

"The hotel, sir?" The driver met his eyes in the rearview mirror, his expression respectful.

He nodded, then sat in silence, hands folded upon his lap, staring out the tinted window to his right.

They left the private airfield and pulled into busy traffic, the long, dark car accelerating smoothly.

"I am worried about you meeting Carlos." Sergei's tone was even and low. "He's slipping away from us. He's part of this somehow, I know it."

He never disputed his security chief's hunches. He could not say the thought had not crossed his own mind. Something was off.

Still, his mind was wandering, not focused on the moment as it should be. He had left a warm bed — and a sleepy, sated Chase in it — and it had almost unbearable to pull himself away. That alone was warning. Never had he felt the pull to remain at someone's side, felt reluctance to part. He frowned disapprovingly. Perhaps it was just the novelty. Surely soon it would die down to something manageable, proper.

He clenched his jaw.

"You made the reservations for me to meet Ren at Bello's, Raymond?"

His aide nodded. "I made it for after the meeting with Carlos. Ren is liable to take this poorly, and I don't want you going into this angry. Carlos is skittish as it is."

He just nodded.

Silence fell for the rest of the trip. The car pulled into the ornate entrance of the Estrada, a luxury hotel he had bought fifteen years ago. It was one of his most lucrative investments, and more to the point, completely free of any drug links. It was part of a chain of holdings that he had cultivated over the years, so that he had properties that could not be traced back to him. If anything happened, these could not be taken away. He wanted all this to be part of a network that would continue on after his own death, providing for Kirith, Laura, Chase, and perhaps now, his own child.

They would never be without financial aid, even if he was no longer here to provide it.

He had reserved here under an assumed name. To them, he would be just another rich business man. Only the elite stayed here, so someone with bodyguards was not out of place. As they pulled up to the front doors, he slid on his sunglasses and stepped out of the car.

"You been good to me, Mr. Martinelli, and it don't seem right, what I seen going down." Carlos was a victim of his own product and obviously in need of it right now. No doubt he had held off to be straight enough to speak to Enzo. The thin man had a shake to his hands, and his eyes darted to and fro, never landing on anything for very long, from Enzo, to Sergei, to Raymond. His fidgeting form was in stark contrast to Enzo's motionless, deadly intensity.

The silence made Carlos worse, and sweat began to bead upon his forehead. "I had to let you know that Santos is pullin' out, bad-mouthing you to the south, but sendin' you messages that everything is good. Don't trust him no more, sir."

"And do you know the reason for Santos's withdrawal? Hear any names? Get a feel for why he feels safe enough to start talking?" Sergei's tone was even enough, but his eyes were dark and intent upon Carlos.

Carlos shrank under the scrutiny, his face now gleaming with moisture. He swallowed hard, then looked pleadingly at Enzo. "I don't know no more than that. Just knew it was important and you had to know."

Enzo leaned back in his chair and reached for a chocolate on the dessert tray next to him. "Good man, Santos. It will be sad to sever our connection so violently. You did well. I'll be sure to see you get another percentage in your take." His tone was even, his expression cold and dark.

Carlos nodded jerkily, his eyes flitting between Enzo and Sergei, trying to avoid Raymond's silent form by the window.

Sergei rose to his feet and jerked his head toward the door.

Carlos shot up as though he were on strings, bowed to Enzo, and scurried in the security chief's wake.

Enzo chewed the chocolate thoughtfully, enjoying the burst of flavor across his tongue. He took his time. He had long ago learned to savor everything in his life, no matter how small. He did not overindulge in anything, choosing instead to enjoy a sensual exploration of surroundings; food, drink, sex. The glory of a sunset, the feel of wind upon his face. Little things.

He had never expected to live this long.

Now someone sought to turn him against a friend. A very good friend. Santos Mendoza had saved his life more than once. When his father had sent him for sniper training down in Peru, with an

allied family. Only fifteen, alone, and desperately missing his
brother, he had started pitting himself against the enemies of the
Mendozas. A family as cold and hard as the Martinellis. And yet,
he had found a friend in Santos, the oldest son, a young man two
years older than him. When Santos was only twenty-one, his father,
Alonzo Mendoza, had been killed and he had taken over
operations in Peru. Santos had worked with Enzo's father, but had
been greatly pleased when the man was killed by Kirith. He had
seen too much of what Enzo had endured under his father's hands.
They were close—very close—and Enzo trusted him completely.
Raymond had come from Santos, an invaluable gift, and now a true
friend.

Sergei returned and sank down into a chair with a grunt,
expression dark.

He eyed him for a moment, before reaching for his glass of
wine.

"Someone is trying to turn me against Santos. Get word to him.
Let him know his security is probably breached and to check the
south connections. See how far this goes." He took a mouthful of
wine, letting it swirl, before swallowing slowly and glancing at
Raymond.

"I want Stacey moved to Italy right away, put in a safe house. I
will explain to her the benefits of agreeing to such a thing."

Raymond nodded, watching him intently.

He put the fragile glass back upon the table, nodding at Sergei.

"Let Carlos deliver his message. Then kill him. You were right.
He is in on this."

Sergei's smile turned feral.

Ren looked up with a brilliant smile as Enzo approached the table,
half rising, until the Martinelli gestured him down. Enzo seated
himself, speaking briefly with the deferential maître d'. The man

smiled, bowing his head respectfully, before leaving.

Their table was in a corner, private and sheltered from the rest of the room, although the other diners could be seen vaguely through the ornate latticework that separated their area.

Ren reached over and laid his hand over Enzo's, stroking over the long fingers.

"I missed you. You would have enjoyed the play. We could still…"

He gave a brief smile, grasping Ren's hand and giving it a small kiss.

"No, amico mio. Sono venuto a parlare."

Ren frowned at something in Enzo's tone, his expression becoming somewhat guarded.

"You came all this way to talk? Must be serious."

"We have always been free with each other. Honest at least, sì?" He met Ren's stare with a faint fond smile.

"Sì." Ren drew back somewhat, searching his face as though for clues.

"We have had good times and have always let each other go when it is time. When things change."

Ren narrowed his eyes, lips thinning. "I would have stayed…"

He shook his head. "You have always had an appetite for the world, amico mio. You would never have been content stuck at my side. You have an amore per la vita. I have always admired that about you. My life would have sucked you dry and bled that out of you. It is good to see that you still possess it."

Ren leaned back in the chair, fingers clenching white over the arms, jaw twitching.

"I don't like the tone of this, Enzo."

"We have been in each other's beds, off and on, for many years. It is not serious, you know that. You have made as much clear to me as well. Last time, it was you who wanted space, who left for France with Thomas."

Ren widened his eyes, and he jerked forward, laying his hand over Enzo's once more.

"That is not true! I feel a great deal for you!"

"Friends. We have always been friends. Even if we cannot live with each other. I regret that I did not contact you more, but time just seemed to…" He shook his head. "I hope that we will continue to be friends, even if we cannot be lovers."

Ren's breath caught.

"If it is something I have done—"

"No, no. You have done nothing wrong. It is more that our timing in getting back together was perhaps not the best."

Ren straightened, eyes narrowing. "That boy, Chase, has something to do with this. He wants you badly. Are you saying that he is…"

Enzo looked up at the waiter as the man offered wine. There was a brief tasting, and a discussion of the merits of the vintage, before both wineglasses were filled and the waiter departed.

He swirled the wine before sipping, his attention returning to Ren.

"It is so." His tone was mild enough, but with the faintest edge of warning that suggested treading carefully.

"So, this is a moment's distraction for you. His youth, his innocence." Ren's tone was neutral, though it was obvious that there was some anger building. Perhaps his ego felt he was being cast aside because of a mere boy…

Enzo paused, gently turning the stem of the wineglass between his long fingers, before he looked up, implacable resolve within his expression.

"He is very important to me." He felt Ren's skepticism. "I will not hurt him. That I swear. He will have no pain from me."

Ren stiffened, jealous tension evident for a split second, before his expression smoothed.

"And how long can this last, Enzo? He is very young for you.

And your life…is he prepared for what you do? What you are?"

Enzo gave a grim smile, a mere tilting of his lips. "Chase has gone through more than you or I will ever know. He is stronger than we could possibly understand." The thread of admiration seemed to make Ren grit his teeth together.

"I see." He lifted his wineglass and drank. "So, I assume this 'talk' is to inform me that I am no longer needed in your bed?" There was a faint bite to the words.

He watched him, feeling a fondness for his hot-tempered friend. "We have never held to each other, Ren. I have never held you back, never tried to chain you."

Ren gave a small, grim smile, then seemed to gather himself.

His expression melted into acceptance, and he raised his wineglass. "A toast then, to your happiness, *amico mio*."

Chapter Nine

Chase hummed to himself as he ate. Half of it was appreciation of Ms. Granger's cooking; the other was joy at the news that Enzo was on his way home. Three days he had been gone, and he had missed him with every breath. His body ached for the Martinelli's touch. He was perpetually aroused at the memories of their time together, and he couldn't sleep for want of that beloved form.

Rafe entered the kitchen and offered him a smile, though it was strained. Ever since it had become known that Chase was now Enzo's lover, Rafe had been odd, stiff, and uncomfortable around Chase, when before their close ages had been a sort of bond between them.

Perhaps Rafe had hoped for more than being merely friends. The thought had crossed his mind before, but such a thing would never have occurred. His heart had been taken long ago, before he met Rafe.

He smiled back, hoping that they could work past this. He had too few friends to be blasé about losing Rafe. Rafe was part of the inner circle, and to be at odds with him would bring a tension into the household, something Enzo would never tolerate. Rafe would be sent elsewhere, a demotion of sorts, and he had no wish to be part of that. Rafe had worked hard to get where he was.

He watched the enforcer wander to the cabinets, pulling out a glass before turning to the fridge, and rummaging for some orange juice.

"I'm sorry I can't be what you want, Rafe," he said softly. The enforcer's back tightened, muscles flexing, then he turned slowly, a dark flush high on his cheekbones, looking at him with incredulous eyes.

"You know?" His voice was harsh with horror.

He kept eye contact, nodding. "I value you as a friend. Please believe that. But that's all it could ever be. I don't want to hurt you, but I have to be honest."

Rafe stared at him for long moments, then lowered his eyes, and a small, wry smile passed over his features. "I always want the ones I can't have. I think I knew from the beginning."

Chase's muscles slowly relaxed as it became clear that Rafe was taking this much better than he had expected. The enforcer's words seemed to point to a history of such relationships, something he could not be held accountable for. It took away some of the guilt.

"Friends though?" He kept his tone even and steady. He wanted to make sure that his demeanor gave no hope to any residual thoughts Rafe may have.

Rafe watched him for long moments, before giving a soft, somewhat sad smile. "If that is all I can have, it's enough. Maybe you can give me tips on how to look for someone who is going to want me back."

He grinned. "I am a pro at unresolved longing. If I can win, then so can you. We'll work on it, you and I."

Rafe nodded, and the moment smoothed over far better than Chase could ever have hoped for.

The enforcer glanced at his watch and stiffened, drinking the juice in a single gulp. "Shit, they're going to be back any second, and I haven't got the vehicle out yet. Sergei will have my balls."

He sprinted out of the kitchen with Chase's surprised laughter floating after him.

He shoveled the last few mouthfuls down his throat, feeling excitement course through this body.

Enzo was coming home.

⌣

Enzo felt an unfamiliar anticipation curl within his stomach as he looked down upon his estate.

Tanglewood.

He had purchased the vast estate from a British millionaire many years ago and adopted the name. It had been built in an Italian style, and he had added to it, modernized it, but left the vast wild-treed grounds as they had been. It sprawled out under his gaze, three courtyards surrounded by porticos, the main building framing around each of them. The pool shone in the sunlight, taking up the fourth courtyard. A beautiful English garden wandered around the south side, with more formal trimmed hedges leading to the huge copper fronted doors of the entrance way. The vast circular driveway matched the size of the enormous house, and to the southwest gleamed a massive man-made lake. To the north, a huge garage complex loomed, with a collection of his priceless cars. East of it, the staff quarters encircled on three sides by the forest, home to all those who lived under his protection.

It was private and peaceful, the electrified fence that surrounded it far away, the guards unseen, a haven for those fortunate enough to live within the warm confines of the estate.

He was always glad to return. His home had always been a bulwark against the world, a place where he could forget the savagery that dwelt within him, the things he did, and the things he ordered others to do.

He could pretend to be normal within the boundaries of his home.

But now there was a new element to the relief he always felt.

Now there was someone waiting for him, loving him in a manner he had never experienced before. Chase did not want his money, his connections, or anything else his world could offer.

Chase wanted him alone.

Enzo had no idea how to deal with such a thing. It was new and fresh, and it made him feel surprisingly young, free in a way he had never known. He had been honed and pressed into what his father wanted from the time he was a child. This feeling of personal freedom was strange, and he was not completely comfortable with it yet. Perhaps never would be. But if Chase was the one to give him this gift, he would tentatively explore it. It seemed that trust went both ways.

He smiled, ever so faintly. Trust was a thing he knew little of. Perhaps his young lover had just as much to teach Enzo as the other way round.

Sergei nudged him with an elbow.

"Good to see you smile for a change. That boy is going to be the making of you. Wait and see."

He rolled his eyes, but could not wipe the happy expression away.

"We'll see."

The helicopter set down with soft precision, barely a jolt, and when the blades had slowed somewhat, two enforcers ran forward, bent down and shielding their eyes from the downdraft. They slid back the door and ushered him out, guiding him past the danger of the blades and to the waiting vehicle. He slid in, Sergei and Raymond close behind, and leaned back against the leather seat, letting out a breath of relief.

He was home.

He had half expected Chase to be in the vehicle, but knew his impatience was unwarranted. Chase would never push himself forward and certainly not at such a new stage in their relationship. He would be at the house, waiting impatiently.

The SUV climbed the steep hill up to the house with powerful ease, and pulled up to the front door. The driver, Rafe, looked over his shoulder at his employer, a familiar grin playing over his lips. "Welcome home, sir."

He nodded to him and exited the vehicle with rather more haste than he was comfortable showing. He slowed his steps, hearing Sergei's annoying chuckle behind him. Raymond took his briefcase from him, a small smile hovering on the edge of his lips, jerking his head slightly to the left.

Enzo followed his assistant's gesture and caught his breath.

Chase stood at the bottom of the massive curving staircase, his face flushed, hands fidgeting restlessly together. He took a step forward, eagerness in every line of his body, then seemed to remember they had an audience, stopping uncertainly.

He stepped past Raymond, his eyes trained on Chase, an almost feral feeling of possession overtaking his senses.

He was his. All his.

Everything else faded but the desire to stake his claim.

Chase was blushing, but his eyes shone as they met his predatory stare.

He grasped Chase's wrist and began to ascend the stairs with swift, impatient steps. Chase stumbled a little, but he pressed close, following with willing eagerness.

He flung open the door to his suite with impatience driving every move. Once within the sanctuary of his rooms, he released Chase, pulling at his own tie with swift efficiency. His gaze pinned Chase with hot need.

"Strip." His usual cool, smooth tone was harsh with repressed lust.

Chase almost tore his T-shirt as he ripped it over his head with swift compliance to the order. His shorts and boxers followed, and then with a boldness foreign to his nature, he took the three steps necessary to bring his naked body flush against Enzo's clothed form, his face canted up, blue eyes bright with want.

They kissed, and Enzo was almost gentle for the briefest of moments, before his feral nature took over, and he growled, biting at Chase's lips, and thrusting his tongue deep within the pliant mouth of his younger lover.

Chase whimpered, standing on his toes, almost climbing Enzo's form in an attempt to press himself closer.

He let his hands stroke down over Chase's lean back, humming in his throat as he cupped rounded buttocks, and forced their rigid erections against each other, flexing his hips, closing his eyes at the rampant need that seemed to overtake all sense of control.

Chase unfastened his suit jacket, pushing it back off Enzo's shoulders with impatient fingers. Dispensing with his usual fastidiousness, he let it fall in a crumpled heap upon the floor, grunting with approval as Chase immediately set to work on difficult shirt buttons.

Far too many of the damn things it seemed to both of them. It was a relief for him to shrug himself free of the impediment, to feel the caress of Chase's long fingers over his chest and stomach, dipping under the waistband of his slacks. He sucked in a shuddering breath. If Chase touched his throbbing cock, it would be over in a matter of seconds.

"On the bed." His voice was a mere husk of sound, his need making him almost incoherent. He could not remember ever being this hot, even in his youth. He had to have Chase, now.

Chase obeyed, scrambling up on the massive bed and laying on his back, one hand grasping his cock with whitened fingers, as though he sought to hold back his own orgasm. Obviously it was not just him who needed this with such intensity.

The way Chase touched himself, the slight unconscious movement of his hips, the way he licked his lips, made him blaze with want. Dear God, but the boy was beautiful.

He unfastened his pants with slow care, feeling the heat rise within him as Chase's eyes followed every movement, heat flushing those pale cheeks. Careful not to touch his own member, he toed his shoes off, before pushing his pants and boxers down with alacrity.

Chase made a small noise in his throat, eyes fixed upon Enzo's cock with such hungry intensity that he gritted his teeth, unbearably turned on by that simple sound.

Two strides, and he was beside the bed, a growl rumbling up through his throat as Chase spread his legs wide, arching himself wantonly, need in every line of his lithe body.

He froze, seeing the unmistakable sign of moisture on Chase's hole.

The little devil…

He grinned, feeling the fire rise in his groin. Reaching for Chase's ankles, he dragged him to the edge of the bed before lifting his legs high and wide, exposing him utterly. Holding Chase's legs in place with one arm, he reached down and directed his cock, rubbing over that enticing entrance, feeling the taut resistance.

"Please," Chase whispered, eyes fixed upon him pleadingly, arms spread wide and fingers clenching upon the sheets.

He pressed forward, trying to restrain his feral side enough to remember that Chase needed some degree of gentleness to become accustomed to sexual activity once more. It took all of his will to go slowly, to sink into that incredible heat in small increments, retreating, then thrusting more deeply. When at last he was balls deep, he stood motionless for long moments, savoring the sensations.

The sound of Chase's small, panting breaths brought him back, and he stared down into that familiar face, a strange sort of possessiveness filling every pore of his being. Stronger than anything he had felt for a lover before. Powerful. He shook his head, seeking to drive the feeling away.

Grasping Chase's ankles up and out, he pulled him more

snugly against his thighs.

Chase's eyes were wide, his gaze fixed on his face as though imprinting every expression his lover made. He rolled his hips, pressing deeper. The slow glide was beyond pleasurable, the tightness of Chase's channel encasing his cock with delicious heat. He could feel the pull on the head of his member with each withdrawal, sensitivity making him gasp, a sound he could never recall making during sex before.

What this boy did to him...

He parted his legs, bracing himself, before driving deeper, a harsh exhale of breath escaping him with each thrust.

Chase writhed on the bed, unable to reach him, incredibly erotic sounds escaping his throat. He stared up at him as though he held every answer, as though he were the sun and moon both.

He could endure the separation no longer and released Chase's legs, setting a knee on the bed, as he pushed his lover further up onto the mattress. Harshly he took Chase's lips, savoring the moans, the way Chase's fingers clutched at him, raking through his hair and then sliding down his back, settling upon his buttocks and pulling feverishly.

Sweat beaded upon his brow, his breath coming in harsh, uneven gusts. He wanted this so much that his usual stamina seemed nowhere in existence. There was so much heat, so much want and need...

Chase arched beneath him, a scream stolen from his lips, as he plundered his mouth, wanting even the sound to be his own.

The sudden tightness, the sweet heat spasming around his cock threw him over the edge of endurance.

With a hoarse moan of completion, he thrust so deep that he drove Chase up the bed, once, twice, then froze in place, arched, head hanging back, his vision going almost white for a moment.

Waves of pleasure crashed over him, each pulling his senses close, then away again, as though he hardly had any control of his body. He trembled, hardly realizing he was doing so, before collapsing to his elbows.

In some corner of his mind, he knew he could not crush Chase, so he pulled out slowly, before rolling to the side, face buried against Chase's neck, each rasping pant drawing in the scent of his lover.

It took time to come back to himself, something that would have worried him before. Now he could not bring himself to care.

Chase gently combed through his hair with a shaking hand, stroking it back from his sweat-soaked forehead.

"I'm so glad you're home." Chase's weak whisper was punctuated with a kiss.

So was he.

He closed his eyes and drew Chase closer with one arm. He might never leave again.

Chase woke, blinking at the sun that spilled through the blinds, and across the bed. He felt so replete, so content...

He widened his eyes as he became more aware, feeling the heat along his back, and the strong arm that lay over his ribs and up his chest.

He curved his lips into a smile, feeling a rush of joy.

Enzo was home. They had made love.

Any doubts and fears that had built up over Enzo's absence were gone. That loving touch had driven them out. His ferocity, force, and need had proven quite thoroughly that he had missed Chase, that it had not been one-sided.

Chase stroked his hand over the arm that held him close.

He would be patient. Today he would ask what had come of Ren, but he knew that Enzo must have done something. There was no chance of Enzo being less than devoted to a single lover. He had seen that all too often, but now that it applied to him, he could only be grateful.

Until the next one took his place.

He squeezed his eyes shut, breath hitching in his chest, then opened them to stare at the sunlight once more. He had known there were no guarantees. He had seen Enzo with his lovers, knew they never held his interest for long. Stacey had been the longest, but then she held the potential for an heir within her.

Chase frowned. He had heard or seen nothing of Stacey since his affair with Enzo had begun. What role would she play now? He swallowed hard, trying to control the wave of jealousy that flowed over him. She could give Enzo a child. What did he have to offer? This would be heaven itself while it lasted, but then…

I love him. She does not.

Would that be enough for Enzo? Would he even recognize what Chase was offering?

He shook the thoughts from himself as though they were annoying flies. He had this moment, more than he had ever believed would come. Now was not the time to worry. He would revel in every touch, in the right to be with Enzo, to call him lover.

Turning slowly, and with care within the circle of Enzo's arm, he settled himself back on his pillow, gaze fastened upon the feast before him.

Enzo lay on his side, one arm under his pillow, the other pinning Chase close. The intimacy of being this close made him blink rapidly. So beautiful, his Enzo. Long, thick lashes shielded those piercing eyes, and his face seemed younger, more innocent, than the vibrancy he showed while awake.

Cautiously, he reached out, giving into the urge to stroke that black hair, to bury his fingers in its softness. He stroked downward, letting his touch linger on the nape of Enzo's neck.

Enzo stirred, lips parting, a whisper of breath feathering over Chase's face. Greatly daring, he shifted his touch, laying his palm over a high cheekbone.

Enzo made a sound, the faintest hum of approval, and turned his face into the touch.

Chase held his breath, wanting to imprint the moment upon his inner eye, so that he would forever have this image.

Enzo had turned to him with instinct, even if it was only in sleep.

He bit his lip, hesitating, then smiled to himself, slipping under the sheet, letting his hands trail over firm muscle and bronze skin. Enzo stretched under his touch and rolled onto his back, one hand under his head, the other flung across his belly, fingers flexing sleepily.

Chase pushed the sheet further back, resenting its intrusion, the way it covered Enzo's hips and hid his beauty from view. Licking his lips, keeping his eyes on Enzo's face, he dipped down, letting his tongue trail over flaccid flesh. Enzo's cock twitched, and he rolled his head upon the pillow, his lips parting ever so slightly, one leg lolling to the side, providing more room for Chase to maneuver. He moaned, the taste exploding over his tongue. It was a bounty, a feast, and he had no idea where to start. His lips trailed down, and he captured a testicle with his lips, mouthing it gently, before sucking it within his mouth, letting his tongue gently lave the tender flesh.

Enzo's body jerked, and he murmured under his breath, eyes still closed, the hand upon his stomach sliding down to comb through Chase's hair, stroking faintly at first, obviously still half asleep, before sinking in, and holding him to his task.

Chase hummed, sucking gently upon soft skin. He drew back, resisting the hand in his hair and blew across the wetness, watching in fascination as the skin moved on its own, reacting to the chill. He glanced up again, meeting half-lidded dark eyes, shivering as he heard the deep moan that escaped his lover's throat.

His own cock hardened at the sound, and he bent his head

again, capturing the other testicle, and drawing it into wet heat. He lapped at it, twining his tongue around the precious orb within, providing enough pressure to make Enzo's hips begin to move in half-dazed reaction.

This he was good at. This he had talent for. He might be ashamed of his past, but at this moment, everything he had learned came to the fore, to please this man he loved so dearly. For this moment, he was confident and heady in his need to please.

"Chase..." The whisper was hoarse, sleepy, and incredibly sexy. He felt goose bumps rise upon his skin at that single sound, his name upon those lips.

He longed to rise, to kiss them, but not yet. First he would drive his lover to need, to show him that he could offer sensuous promise—and deliver total satisfaction. He would bring what weapons he had to bear, and he would keep Enzo as long as he could.

Forever, if he could only have his way.

He let the second testicle slide from his mouth, and Enzo's faint groan seemed to indicate some sort of sleepy protest. He nipped his way up, so gently using his teeth to torment, to bring to the edge of pain, and yet never over. Reaching up, he grasped the half-hard cock that beckoned him and applied his tongue to the circumcised skin just below the head, knowing how tender and sensitive it was. The tip of his tongue traced under the corona, lapping at its edge, hearing a hiss of breath and looking up to witness Enzo waken fully, his head arching back, his free hand clutching at the sheets.

Precum beaded upon the tip, glistening in the sunlight, and he touched it gently with his tongue, his eyes sliding shut with bliss at the taste. The primal part of him was fascinated, taking Enzo's essence within his mouth, swallowing it, having it become part of him. He closed his lips over the head, sucking gently, seeking more of the slickness that Enzo's body was offering to him.

Enzo groaned, a long, low sound, before powerful hands

grasped Chase and pulled him up over Enzo's body, his head canting eagerly to meet the kiss that awaited. Enzo arranged him, so that he straddled the dark-skinned body. He felt the press of that thick cock against his entrance, and shifted his hips, not wanting gentleness.

His whimpering moans seemed to drive Enzo into a darker need. He shifted before thrusting deep.

Chase arched, his lover's hands gripping his waist, steadying him as he cried out at the piercing, a wail of pleasurable pain that made his senses burn and pulse. The remains of last night's loving eased the way to a degree, and the burn of harsh entry faded swiftly into hot intensity. He swiveled his hips, loving the sense of pressure within him, the feel of Enzo's cock pressing, gliding over his prostate with delicious friction. Licking his lips, he looked down into dark brown eyes that gleamed in the light, the look of an awakened predator. Enzo's hands grasped Chase's hips, pulling him down sharply each time he rose up to the tip of that thick, hard shaft.

He whimpered at the sensations, the force that spoke to something deep within him. This is what he had always needed, he suddenly realized. Pleasure with a spike of pain, a lover he could trust not to take things too far. And trust he did, despite Enzo's reputation for wildness. Some instinct that told him he need never worry that Enzo's feral nature would harm him. The Martinelli would never injure those he cared for, and at this moment in time, for however long it might last, Enzo cared for him.

That was all Chase needed. More than that, he could not imagine.

Enzo watched as Chase leaned across the table, accepting the piece of peeled juicy peach with a hum of appreciation, lingering to suck Enzo's fingers clean, before sinking back into his chair with hot eyes trained on his lover.

Enzo licked his own fingers to remove any remnants of juice, his gaze fixed unerringly upon Chase, watching the blue eyes widen, the pupils dilate with lust at the sight.

Enzo chuckled under his breath. "Down, boy. You have worn me out. Last night, this morning — you are insatiable."

"You make me that way. How do I look at you, and not want to touch, to taste? It's completely your fault." Chase muttered around his piece of peach.

His eyebrow rose. "I have not had this problem with other lovers."

"Then they were both blind and stupid, and probably knowing you, you were the one who kicked them out of your bed first thing in the morning, wanting to sleep in peace." Chase's expression held a hint of mischief, an expression Enzo treasured on his young lover.

"I would not be so crass." He smirked. At the disbelieving look Chase gifted him with, he laughed out loud, deftly using his knife to slice the remains of the peach into neat sections. He slid one into his mouth, humming at the sweet juice that exploded over his tongue.

Chase leaned forward, eyes intent, boldly laying a hand on Enzo's jaw, and tilting his head to lick the juice from his lover's lips with long, slow sweeps of his tongue.

Enzo kissed him, the sweetness of peach shared between them.

It was long moments before Chase withdrew, smiling, his expression filled with contentment, as he sat back in his chair, and once more picked up his spoon, working on the cereal he had been eating before Enzo introduced peaches.

Enzo watched him fondly, feeling a languid peace steal over him. There was no sense of urgency, no need to break the moment with sexual fervor. This feeling was almost — comfortable — as though the relationship completed something, filled some gap or space within him that had been waiting.

It was so strange, and yet, he could not find the energy to question it. It simply was. It made him wonder why he had taken so damn long to see what Chase could be to him.

The worries were still there, buried, along with a heightened desire to protect the younger man, but in all, he could not bring himself to take away from the pleasant calm that seemed to envelop them both. It was as though this were right and good in a way that he seldom encountered.

This held none of the taint of his work, none of the jaded cynicism for people's motives that always colored his dealings with others. Chase had joined a very select few that he trusted enough to relax with. Somehow the boy had wormed his way into Enzo's mind and heart, and for the moment, he found he could not regret that.

He wanted to linger in this moment for as long as possible, as though nothing unpleasant waited outside their intimate haven.

What would it be like to be normal, to have this on a daily basis?

He shook off the introspection, not wanting unpleasant reality to intrude on their time together. For this moment, he was just a man with his lover.

"I spoke with Ren. You need not worry about his return. He understood in his own way. We have been friends a long time, lovers off and on again. There are no promises on either side, although more often it was him who sought freedom."

Chase stopped chewing for a long moment, eyeing him in silence, before swallowing his cereal and licking his lips, making Enzo's thoughts scramble most pleasantly.

"I think he may have a little more invested in you then you think. He seemed more fixated on you than a casual fuck buddy." Chase's tone held a quiet certainty that made Enzo frown slightly.

"Ren will play with your mind if you give him half a chance. He never takes anything terribly seriously." He hoped that Chase would understand.

Chase nodded after a moment, but Enzo could see that he was not convinced. He thrust the situation away. Ren was gone for the moment, and if this new relationship with Chase continued, then his friend would have to come to terms with the present way of things. That was that.

"I have sent Stacey to Italy, to a house of mine where she can be protected, until the baby comes and we determine paternity." He could hear that faint relief in his own voice, somewhat surprised by the level of release he found in her absence. She had become more of a liability than he had quite noticed. The notion of marrying her to legitimize any children seemed more distasteful than he remembered. It seemed being with Chase changed a great many of his viewpoints, the realization making him uneasy in a way he was unfamiliar with.

He forced himself back to calm. This was just new. Things needed to settle into a comfortable pattern, and he would be back on solid ground once more. It was no more than that, nothing to fret upon.

He leaned forward to claim a milky kiss.

Chapter Ten

The first bullet slammed into the Jaguar with a high-pitched whine, and the second shot sounded hard on its heels, but Chase only felt the pain as a sharp sting, as he was flung to the ground, Enzo covering him with his own body, cursing virulently in Italian, shouting at his bodyguards. Chase lay there, stunned, the chaos exploding around him in slow motion. The pain in his shoulder began to escalate, but he gritted his teeth and lay still under his lover, not wanting Enzo distracted.

It had been such a lovely evening. They had attended a high-profile gathering of celebrities, within whose ranks Enzo seemed intimately connected, and very at ease despite the presence of media, and in all probability, police.

Chase had struggled to live up to his own expectations of what he thought Enzo's lover should be, but Enzo had soon taken him aside and told him to be himself. If he didn't wish to speak, he didn't have to. If he wanted to meet a certain celebrity or join a discussion Enzo was having, he had only to indicate so, and Enzo would see it done. In other words, he had the control.

It eased him, and he found himself listening, watching, fascinated by this otherworldly phenomenon of vast wealth and influence, and the unreal people who moved within its circles. He surprised himself with the calm aura he managed to project, Enzo's presence giving him courage. There had been no raised eyebrows, no malicious glances, and it soon became apparent that Enzo held sway here in a way that he would not have expected. People seemed glad to see him, whether in honesty, or in an attempt to flatter the Martinelli, but either way, Enzo hardly needed to circulate. Everyone came to him.

He saw his lover in a different light, for in this atmosphere, Enzo did not seem the drug lord; he meshed with those around him with envious ease, a smooth charm in his smile, ease in his voice. He did not seem to have the tense predator energy that seemed so prevalent with other parts of his life.

If Chase hadn't known his background, he would have simply seen Enzo as a rich member of this elite society.

He watched him quietly, a little wistfully. This was what Enzo could have been if he not been imprinted almost from birth into violence. In whatever he would have done otherwise, he would have ended up here. He was too clever and driven to be anything but successful. Chase sipped champagne and wished for a way to work his lover free of what bound him. How much of Enzo was the predator who had no conscience, who gloried in violence, and how much was a man who could walk away from it?

That was the truth of it. Much though he prayed for a future, the fact was that Enzo lived a life of violence, and in all likelihood, would die as he had lived. Who was Chase to change the ways of a lifetime? He might love Enzo to his very soul, but he was helpless in the face of reality, and that reality was that Enzo was comfortable with death in all its forms in a way that Chase couldn't fathom. He didn't fear death, couldn't, after all he had faced as a child and youth, but he saw no need to dance with it, as Enzo did.

If only…

They had left the event at a reasonable hour, and Enzo had directed the driver to a restaurant that he knew well, having bought a share in the business some years ago.

The owners, an older Italian couple, greeted him with exuberance and obvious delight, with nothing of fear in it. Chase warmed to them immediately, and they seemed delighted that Enzo was with such a beautiful young man, who was so shy and blushed at their praise.

Enzo had smiled and guided him to an outdoor table that overlooked the harbor, lights glinting off the rippling water. The night breeze was warm and gentle, laden with the scent of nearby nocturnal blooms, and he soaked it in, wishing to imprint every detail upon his mind's eye. This was all so beautiful, with a sense of unreality about it, like an old romantic tale.

It was not hard to see Enzo as his hero.

His lips quirked a little sadly. If only his white knight didn't head a drug dynasty. Somehow that tarnished the image.

He chastised himself harshly. He loved Enzo despite everything, yet here he was spending the entire evening envisioning Enzo as something he could never be. Even if there was something within the Martinelli that would even want such freedom, it was a well-known fact that the only way out of Enzo's position was death itself. The very dogs that looked up to him now, would tear him apart, seeing his retreat as weakness.

Chase shuddered, feeling as though premonition ghosted over his skin.

Enzo turned away from the waiter, shooting a look of concern at his young lover. "Are you chilled? Do you wish to move to a table inside?"

He shook his head, feeling a frisson of joy at the degree of caring Enzo was displaying. It was not normal behavior for the Martinelli, so to receive it was an indication of favor that made Chase's toes curl in reaction. "I am fine," he responded quietly, reaching across the table to capture Enzo's fingers. "Thank you."

Enzo studied him for a long moment, no doubt to satisfy himself that he was telling the truth, before relaxing back in his chair. His thumb traced over the back of Chase's knuckles with almost absentminded fondness, warmth radiating up his arm from the welcome touch.

The food was fantastic, the scenery breathtaking, with the lights, the water, the soft sound of waves against the pier. They had taken their time, talking about various topics, laughing now and then. Chase wanted to imprint every moment, wanted to hold this within him forever.

It all felt so unbelievably perfect.

Then they had left the restaurant.

Sergei had been waiting at the entrance, two other men at his side, and they had guided Enzo and Chase to one of the waiting cars. It had only been a few steps.

Now he lay there, cheek pressed against the cold concrete, feeling the pain radiate and spread.

A whimper broke free, and he felt Enzo's arm tighten around him. Fear for Enzo's safety rose in his thoughts, and he tried to speak. He found it hard to focus on the noise around them both, everything seemed to be swimming, and he gave a little sigh of surprise as his senses faded into darkness.

Sergei stood at attention near the doorway, wary eyes fixed upon the Martinelli, Raymond waiting at his shoulder, face showing no expression.

Enzo had not spoken since the shooting, had remained silent through the rush home, the call for one of their doctors, Chase's subsequent treatment.

Silence was never a good thing when dealing with the Martinelli. Silence was a sign of the rising darkness within Enzo, the near madness that haunted the Martinelli line.

Enzo paced, slowly, and with great control, another bad sign.

Temper and action released anger, this frightening control only increased the fury boiling within. Sergei had no desire to take the brunt of what would boil over given an outlet, any outlet. When Enzo was at his worst, his darkness seemed to have great difficulty recognizing friend from foe. It was his job to keep his boss under wraps enough to prevent any incidents that Enzo would regret later. Raymond's job was to work past the anger, soothe it down to manageable levels.

Not an easy task.

Enzo paced with his eyes fixed upon the setting sun framed through the doors to the balcony of his bedroom. He did not watch as the doctor cleaned, stitched, and dressed Chase's wounds, front and back of his right shoulder, just below the collarbone.

It was a blessing that Chase stayed unconscious, because Sergei was quite sure that Enzo's false calm would never have held through the boy crying out in pain. For the doctor's sake, he hoped that whatever he had given the boy would remain potent until the job was done, and the doctor long gone.

It was eerily quiet in the room, only the sound of the doctor's movements bringing any relief to the potent silence. Sergei had to remind himself to breathe. His mind was racing with the events of the evening, most of his attention on the priority of protecting the Martinelli and his lover, the rest on the orders he had given two of his finest men: to trace the shooter. He had given no information to anyone else. The timing, the swift efficiency of the hit was obvious. This had not been to kill; this had been to warn.

And the Martinelli did not take a warning well.

He had his suspicions about the shooting, but he would keep his mouth shut until Enzo chose to speak with him, or his men returned with concrete evidence.

The doctor began to pack up his supplies, and Enzo whirled, attention pinpointing the man immediately. The doctor had been working for the Martinellis for a great many years. He kept his eyes lowered, his posture submissive, moving with slow sure actions, nothing to provoke the beast.

"The wound was a clean in and out. His bleeding cleansed the site well. I have cleansed it further, stitched it. I want you to keep an eye out for infection. Call me if you have the faintest doubt." He pulled the covers up over Chase's still form. "I have given the boy something for pain and to make him sleep, so he should be out until the morning at least. I'll leave some pills here; pain, sleep aids, and antibiotics. They're labeled. Is there anything else you want from me? Was anyone else hurt?" His brief look encompassed the blood that stained Enzo's shirt.

He shook his head, gesturing the doctor to him as he opened the door. "Just the boy. Thanks, Darell, for coming out so late."

"I don't think you lot have ever called me during the day. I'm used to it by now." Darell's voice held wry humor, but he shot a look of concern back into the room. "You're sure none of that blood is his?"

"Believe me, I checked Enzo over immediately." Both men shared a look, knowing exactly how difficult Enzo would have made that examination, with his temper up and his lover injured.

"I'll come by tomorrow evening, make sure the boy is doing well." Darell shook Sergei's hand, then walked away in the company of Raymond. Nobody was being trusted at this point.

Sergei reentered the room, closing the door softly behind him.

Enzo had crossed to the bed and was standing silently, staring down at Chase, his face utterly inscrutable. His hands slowly clenched into fists, before he whirled on his heel, and stalked out upon the balcony. Fingers flexed upon the stone railing, the muscles in his jaw working with his thoughts.

Sergei hesitated, then slowly approached, until he could sink into his chair, trying to make his muscles relax as he watched his friend, his boss.

It was a half hour or more before Enzo finally took a deep breath.

"I want you to bring Benito here." The tone was harsh, those dark eyes filled with a bottomless rage. "I think it is time I spoke to my uncle."

Sergei knocked upon his boss's office door. He tried to shake off the grim expression on his face.

"Come in, Sergei." Enzo's voice sounded more controlled now.

Sergei swung open the heavy walnut door, stepping inside first, so Benito Martinelli would have to pass him.

Benito, heavyset and broad, lacking Enzo's height and fine features, stepped into the lush office with commendable poise, but with wariness clear in his small, dark eyes. Sergei saw the man size up every corner of the room. That was the first thing these Martinellis always did.

Enzo was leaning back in his chair, relaxed, calm.

"*Benvenuto, Zio.*" He gestured to a comfortable chair stationed before the great desk.

Sergei gave a brief nod to his boss and began to retreat from the doorway.

"Stay, Sergei." Enzo set his glasses upon the desk. "There's a gunman on the loose. I'm sure my uncle will feel more comfortable knowing that you are right beside him. Please, close the door."

Sergei did as he was asked. He took up position beside Benito and folded his arms across his chest.

A coldness was evident in Benito's eyes. He was definitely not happy to have company. "*Nipote. Buona per vedere.*"

Benito seated himself, crossing one leg over the other and resting his interlaced hands over his knee.

"My nephew, I have to say that I am very sorry to hear of the shooting. I trust the young man is recovering well?" Nothing in the tone but polite concern.

Enzo watched him for a long, silent moment, his stare piercing, before he nodded in acceptance of the statement. "He is strong. The wound was clean through."

"Good, good. I am glad to hear it." Benito's stare never wavered. "I am puzzled though as to why you would wish to see me so soon after the incident."

Enzo sat forward, elbows upon the desk, hands clasped over each other, viewing Benito with seemingly polite intensity.

"I have a proposition for you."

Benito tilted his head slightly, curling the corner of his mouth in a cold smile. "You wish me to find out if Paolo had some hand in this?"

Enzo frowned at him, showing no anger or surprise at the comment.

"I have no need of such a thing. I am, instead, offering you a chance to step into my position."

Benito's body tightened, and he leaned forward ever so slightly, a look of disbelief on his face. Sergei caught himself spellbound by this turn of events too. He straightened his back. What game was Enzo playing here?

"Why would you do this?" Benito's expression morphed into suspicious enquiry.

Enzo leaned back, a weariness seeming to take possession, lining his face.

"I have led this family for a long time. I find myself wanting something different, something without having to watch my back every moment."

Benito watched him in silence for long moments. "This shooting rattled you. The boy is more important to you than I would have thought." His look was calculating.

Enzo shrugged. "Perhaps it is him. Perhaps not. This has been in my thoughts for much longer than he has been in my life. This kind of life, it wears upon me. Does it not, Sergei?"

Sergei grunted. He knew he was not expected to contribute

anything to this discussion other than his silent, hulking presence. That was enough.

Enzo gave a small smile. "These days, I cannot even have a friendly chat with my own family members, in my own house, without a bodyguard present. I grow weary of these games."

Benito's expression showed a sneer for the briefest of moments, contempt in his gaze as it alighted upon Sergei's gun holster. The man was not a fool. He knew what Sergei's presence implied.

"Your father would not have been pleased to see you step aside from your duties."

Something cold and dark flickered across Enzo's face, and Benito looked aside, briefly, not encouraging aggression.

"I have no concern whether my father would have approved or not. He is no longer here. My decisions only need to make sense to me alone. If you are not interested, I am more than willing for it to pass down to Paolo."

Benito shifted in his seat. "I am simply concerned by this sudden desire to vacate your position."

"It will not be immediate. I wish to offer you the chance to step up and show me what you are capable of. I will give you responsibility for the large sectors of the business, and you can go from there. If you show promise and strength of leadership, it will be all yours in a year."

Avarice ghosted over Benito's face. "Why not Paolo?" His suspicions were clear within his expression.

"You are the eldest, after my father. You have the right. From what my sources tell me, you could lead the family well."

Benito straightened, a hint of surprise in the movement. "I had not thought you noticed."

"I always notice strength in any of the family. You have wanted more power for a very long time. I am offering it to you. Though you might want to do something about your youngest son, Ilario. He is a fool."

Benito stared, then nodded, face twitching with inner thoughts. It was clear he was suspicious, but his greed, his jealousy of his nephew leading the family was acting against rationality.

"I would be able to work on the southern territories then?" His desire for the most lucrative areas of the business were clear.

"If you accept, I will inform our contacts, and you can show me how you would like things to be run. If it seems to work well, then you can have them."

Benito almost vibrated, his lust for becoming head of the family almost palatable. "And Paolo?"

"That will be up to you. I know you two are close, so you can include him as you see fit. You could even co-rule if that would please you." Swift rejection flashed over Benito's expression. Sergei had to forcibly stop himself from laughing out loud. There was nothing better than watching Enzo play with his uncle's emotions like this.

"And you? What will you do if I take over?" Benito's contempt was barely hidden.

"I have my wealth. I need no more. I will live as I see fit."

"With your boy?" The sneer drew up Benito's lip.

Sergei tensed. That was the wrong thing to say.

Enzo leaned forward, cold malice in every inch of his body.

"Speak of him in such a manner again, *Zio*, and you will see why I was chosen for leadership when you were not. I would hate to have to kill a family member, but you will not disrespect me. Leader or not, I would have your balls, and you know it."

Benito shifted back in the chair, turning his gaze aside once more, sullen compliance evident in his manner.

"If you start showing any belligerence toward me during this trial period, I can and will pass it over to Paolo. You are not indispensable, by any means. I am giving you a chance for something you have always wanted. Use the opportunity well, and you will have it. Start raising my anger, and you will gain nothing.

Is that clear?"

Benito drew a deep breath, a vein throbbing on the side of his neck. Sergei actually heard the man's teeth grinding with displeasure at being chastised by his nephew. Finally, he nodded. The tension in the room seemed to ebb away, and Sergei felt the muscles in his shoulders relax for the first time in several minutes.

"I will do as you ask, *nipote*."

"Good. I will speak with our contacts, and let them know of the changes. I think you will do well, *Zio*, and the Martinellis will stay strong beneath your leadership."

A hint of surprise and pleasure flashed over Benito's face. Both men stood and Benito reached out, meeting Enzo's hand halfway. The handshake was firm, and Sergei fancied he could see that each was applying more force than necessary.

A brief look from Enzo told Sergei that it was time to escort the man out of the office. They would not be sharing a drink in celebration. The meeting was over.

He opened the door and moved aside for Benito, who was grinning from ear to ear. Pulling the door closed behind him, Sergei caught a glimpse of Enzo's face. He was smiling too. But it was the cold, razor-sharp smile of a shark.

Chase woke with a soft groan of pain, blinking dazedly at the ornate ceiling of Enzo's bedroom. For long moments, he could not imagine where he was or why he hurt so badly. Then memory crashed over him, and he gasped, one hand rising to his shoulder. His fingers met thick bandages, and he froze. It was real then. The shooting…not just a horrible dream. Memories of the terrible, biting pain rose, and he thrust them away.

The present pain was duller, a deep ache, and it only flared when he was foolish enough to move that shoulder.

He relaxed into the bed, trying to restrain his need to sit up, to search for Enzo. The last memory he had was of his lover covering him, protecting him. Had Enzo been hurt as well? The mere thought made him shudder, the pain sparking with the movement.

He gritted his teeth, taking deep breaths to control the sensations. He was used to pain, had lived with it as a daily occurrence while under Marcello's ownership. He was no wilting flower to buckle under this wound, but neither was he so foolish as to seek more pain.

When he could breathe properly again, he turned his head slowly, his heart quickening as he saw a large figure lounging upon the leather sofa near the windows, the soft sound of the TV slowly entering his dazed senses.

He sagged in disappointment as he realized it was Sergei. The captain of the enforcers sat in profile to Chase, and the sight of him, hair tousled, body slouching into the comfort of the couch, made him smile. The man looked so different at ease, so rumpled, and almost normal. Not his usual stark perfection and cold demeanor by any means.

Some instinct made Sergei frown, and he turned his head to meet Chase's sleepy eyes.

A smile broke over the guard's harsh features, and Chase felt warmth infuse him. Sergei rose and crossed over to him, the smile still in evidence, a softness to the normally cold eyes.

"So you finally wake! I thought you had perhaps gone into hibernation, boy."

He gave a small grin in reply. He tried to speak twice, before his voice sounded more than a raven's croak.

"Enzo?"

Sergei reached toward the bedside table, bringing a glass of water with a straw into view. Tipping it slightly he managed to bring it to Chase's lips without spilling any.

Chase sipped it slowly, closing his eyes in bliss, as his throat absorbed the moisture gratefully.

When he gestured that it was enough, Sergei withdrew the glass, watching him with the hint of a smile.

"Enzo is on the phone at the moment. He was here all night. Looks like hell, the idiot. Would not sleep for worry of you. Had me here too, to keep him company and help guard you. He is a little protective right now. Like he cares about you, deeply."

He flushed, smiling. "He is all right? He did not get hurt?'

Sergei grinned. "He always seems to come out all right. It is the rest of us who get the bullets, isn't it?" He raised his shirt a few inches. The scars of two bullets were on his right side, the mutilated skin twisted and pale with age.

"Now you are one of us, hmm?" The amusement in Sergei's tone was evident.

"I was hardly protecting him," he argued weakly. "They were targeting me, weren't they? I could have gotten him killed."

Sergei's smile faded. "They were after you. But they were pros. If it was Enzo they were after, they would not have missed. They shot you in the shoulder. It was a warning, no more than that."

Chase shifted slightly, grimacing. "Couldn't they just send a text message?"

Sergei shrugged, tilting his lips slightly. "Call them old-school. Some people in our business are just traditionalists."

"Ha, ha," He put one elbow under him and tried to sit up.

Sergei tsk-tsked, and with surprisingly gentleness, he propped Chase up carefully with well-placed pillows.

He sat with his head back for long moments, letting the pain settle in this new position, before he looked at Sergei once more, thanking him.

"Is Enzo angry?' His voice held a small degree of his former timidity, and it grated upon him. He never wanted to return to the scarred and terrified soul who had first come here. Chase had fought too long and hard to submit to that part of himself ever again.

Sergei shrugged in answer. "With those who did this, yes. With you, no. He cares deeply for you, whether he will ever admit it to himself or not. And you, in turn, could be the making of him."

Chase could only stare at him in disbelief. "No one makes anything of the Martinelli. Nobody influences him to change. If he chooses to do something, it is because he wants to."

Sergei grinned, something that lightened his features and made him look years younger. "You have a great deal of influence, my boy. Never doubt that. It is the fact that you love him that gives you the power. Whether he realizes it or not, he craves that. He trusts you in a fashion that very, very few receive."

Chase flushed, looking down and pleating the edges of the bedcovers. "I don't want power over him. I just want to love him. He needs love." His embarrassment deepened. Who was he to say such things to Enzo's security chief? Then again, it was Sergei who had brought up love in the first place. Who would have thought that the large man held such sensitivity and understanding beneath a harsh expression and large, scarred body? His words made it very evident how much he loved and respected Enzo. Chase had known them to be friends, but he had never suspected the depth of it.

"And that is why you will succeed where so many others have failed. You have brought what he has always needed. A selfless love…a true care of him."

Chase allowed a faint grin to tug at his lips. "You could be on *Oprah*."

Sergei snorted, folding his arms over his massive chest. His glare was softened by the smile lingering in his eyes.

"Cheeky little bastard, aren't you? At least you'll give Enzo a run for his money. Don't let him ever cow you. He won't respect you if you back down all the time."

Chase grimaced. "I am not the best at standing up for myself. You know that."

"You are strong in yourself, or you wouldn't have survived all you have. He respects that, having watched you struggle. I'm not suggesting you argue with him, but make your viewpoint known in your own way. He will listen, even if he doesn't always act on your words."

Chase nodded seriously, biting his lower lip as he considered Sergei's advice. It made sense, and he did not want to be nothing but a shadow in Enzo's life. Enzo would forever label him as too young if he did. He had to find a way to make the Martinelli forget about the age difference.

To realize that, despite everything, they were meant to be together.

Sergei brought him food, soup and crackers, and he managed to get most of it down before he began to nod off. He frowned in annoyance at his exhaustion, but Sergei gave him a long lecture on how to recover from bullet wounds, and he must have fallen asleep in the middle of it.

He woke gradually, a smile spreading over his lips as he felt a beloved presence close by.

"Enzo," he whispered, opening his eyes slowly, joy suffusing him at the closeness of his lover.

Enzo lay beside him, fully dressed, his head propped on one hand, his face serious and closed, eyes expressionless.

Chase ignored it all, leaning forward to lay a kiss upon those lips. For long moments, there was no response, and then Enzo laid him carefully back upon the pillows, and kissed him, soft and sweet, so at odds with his expression.

Chase hummed with pleasure, using his good arm to draw his lover closer. They kissed slowly, languorously, with nothing of haste or sex within it. The tenseness that made Enzo's body stiff and resistant gradually faded, and Chase felt a glow of victory that he could distract his lover from what had occurred.

Enzo traced his long fingers over Chase's features, a silent indication of what lay within his thoughts.

"I'm fine, Enzo. Still here." Chase didn't even try to lighten the words, didn't smile, or try to tease. This was too deep for that, Enzo too on edge.

"They will pay for what they have done." Enzo's whisper held dark promise.

Chase returned the touch, stroking Enzo's lean cheek with his fingers and slowly sliding up into his thick hair. He pulled his lover closer once more, kissing Enzo's face, mapping each feature with loving care, his heart swelling with the realization that he could do this now, could show his feelings with touch and taste.

Enzo allowed the familiarity, but his eyes did not soften, even if his body had relaxed. The darkness within was in full force, thankfully not directed at Chase himself.

Chase closed his eyes, shivering, burying his face against Enzo's broad shoulder, as he was gently pulled into the safety of a full embrace.

He didn't wish to think of what would come of this and the blood that would be shed in his name.

Chapter Eleven

It took a whole week before Chase felt well enough to rise from the bed. He woke to morning sun upon his cheek, the curtains to the balcony pulled back, and the doors wide open. He yawned and stretched, a smile slowly curving his lips. If the doors were open, then it could only mean Enzo was still here, a strange occurrence so late in the morning hours. He rose slowly, grimacing a bit at the pull on his shoulder, before padding to the balcony dressed in only light sleeping pants hanging low on his hips.

He blinked in the sunlight, lifting his face to its warmth with appreciation. If the shooting had done nothing else, it had made him aware of life, of the little things that made each moment wonderful.

He turned his head, taking in the sight of his lover with a small smile.

Enzo was sitting in his chair, bare-chested, bare feet up on a low stool, his laptop open across his thighs. A frown tilted his eyebrows, and it was some moments before he seemed to become aware of Chase's presence, and looked up from his work.

Chase strolled closer, leaning to kiss those stern lips, pleased when they relaxed beneath his, returning the gesture.

Enzo raised his right hand, threading his fingers through Chase's thick hair and teasingly rubbing the scalp with slow, almost sensuous movements.

He groaned ever so slightly, tilting his head like a cat.

Enzo broke the kiss, his gaze sweeping over his features, no doubt cataloging his health as he did so often these days. Chase huffed a breath of resignation, straightening up, regretting the loss of the blissful hand in his hair.

Enzo pulled a chair close, then gestured him into it.

He obeyed, relaxing into the softness with a sleepy groan of appreciation. Faintly he heard Enzo on the phone, ordering breakfast, but he simply reached out and snagged his lover's free hand, entwining their fingers.

Enzo ended the call, placing the phone back on the table before turning his full attention upon Chase.

"You look much better this morning." It was half a question.

"As long as I don't move the shoulder much, you would hardly ever know I was shot." Chase's tone held a hint of teasing.

Enzo frowned, eyes darkening for a moment before he slid the laptop onto the table. He leaned forward and captured Chase's lips once more with more force this time, leaving him humming with arousal by the time they were done.

He blinked rather dazedly, wondering why Enzo had stopped, only to blush furiously as he realized that there were others present, even as their breakfast was set upon the table with brisk efficiency.

He gave a small scowl in Enzo's direction, as Enzo's lips twitched with amusement at his embarrassment.

"Eat. Time enough for lust-filled sex later."

Chase wanted to slide off the chair. He did not think he could be redder. How was it possible that after everything he had endured, this man had the power to make him flush like a teenager? His scowl deepened.

Enzo laughed, a bright clear sound in the morning air, and Chase could only watch, fascinated. God, he was in love with this man, even shame a distant thing if he could bring humor to his lover.

Dark eyes twinkled with rare amusement as Enzo brought Chase's fingers to his lips in a quixotic gesture of fondness. "You are so easy to tease, my boy. It is almost *too* tempting."

"I doubt you are restraining yourself," he grumbled, though he was unable to keep the corners of his mouth from twitching. The kitchen staff was leaving, much to his relief.

"Oh, it could be much, much worse. Ask Kirith sometime about how his big brother has tortured him over the years."

Chase filed that information away for future study. He had a hard time imagining Enzo as a boy, with all the inclinations of youth. Had he ever been carefree, innocent? Or had his family, his father, taken that from him so early he had never got a chance to be a child at all? Chase wanted to snatch that child away, protect him from the future.

He blinked, pulled from his thoughts as Enzo leaned past him to grasp a large mug of coffee. The Martinelli took a first sip, closing his eyes in deep appreciation and licking his lips as he finished.

Chase shook his head at his own fascination. Was it remotely healthy that he was feeling hot and bothered by such a simple thing? Boy, he had it bad.

Enzo shot him a look that was filled with far too much knowledge, pulling his hand free. "Eat. You are too thin as it is."

Chase rolled his eyes, but sat forward, mouth beginning to water at the smell of fresh bacon and a perfectly turned omelet. All of a sudden he was ravenously hungry.

As usual, Enzo ate in fits and starts, perusing his laptop beside his plate with a frown of concentration, sometimes muttering under his breath in impatient Italian.

Chase finished first and sat back with a contented sigh of repletion, sipping his orange juice and enjoying the moment.

Everything was peaceful, and he soaked in the sun after a week of being stuck in bed. The breeze was light on his face, rippling the surface of the lake below, and the soft cries of birds upon the water soothed his nerves. He reached out with his good arm, resting his fingers upon Enzo's thigh with nothing of sexual intent, only the need to feel his lover linked with him.

"If you could, would you find a different way of living, something that would keep you safe for me?" Chase froze, unable to believe he had voiced that aloud.

Beside him, Enzo had stopped abruptly in his typing, and Chase could sense his stare upon him.

Oh dear God, what had he done?

"I'm sorry," he whispered, unable to face his lover. "That was a stupid thing to say."

"To speak from the heart is never foolish. If I were a better man, I could give you your wish." Enzo's tone held a bitterness, a certain degree of self-denigration.

Chase turned in the chair, drawing Enzo down for a kiss, stroking a lean cheek with loving fingers. "You give me so much. I am greedy for wanting anything else."

Enzo watched him with weariness evident in his expression. "This is one of the concerns that I voiced before. You are so young. I want you to live life free of…" He paused, frowning.

"The family?" he questioned, an edge of dislike in his tone. "I hate what they did to you. I want more for you, want to love you until the end of time, not wait for a call that tells me you've been shot." He raised his hand to his own shoulder, the imagery of such a thing happening to Enzo making him physically ill.

"The violence of the Martinelli line would have insured I would have led such a life sooner or later. I was never a good person, Chase, no matter your fantasies. I killed my first man at fourteen, tortured a man at sixteen. By your age, I was a seasoned assassin, and believe me, some of my targets did not deserve death."

He took Enzo's right hand and stroked his fingers over it. "But the drugs—why? Don't you see what it does?" This above all things bothered him.

Enzo drew back a little, quirking a brow. "Should I worry about those who choose to take substances harmful to themselves? I see no need to feel sympathy for stupidity." He shrugged. "I supply what they want. I do not force them to take it. It is what my father did, what will be done long after my time."

"Sometimes it is not so simple. I had a friend on the street. His mother was an addict. The moment he had the smallest trace of cocaine, he was too."

Enzo sat back, expression cooling. "He made the choice to take that first hit. No other. You ask me to care for people. That is not in me. Don't try to give me sentiments that don't exist. People mean nothing to me."

Chase felt his breathing hitch. He knew there was more to Enzo, but how to prove it to a man who had been born and bred to be exactly what he was? He had been taught to be without emotion, to foster nothing but brutal leadership. Violence nurtured a state of mind that held everyone not of his family to be enemy. Yet, he loved, whether he realized it or not. There was emotion within him, a sliver of humanity that had not been destroyed despite his father's best efforts. If Chase could get him away from this influence, show him a world where everyone was not a potential threat, could there be hope that Enzo might possibly turn from violence, and find a different path?

It would take a miracle. And he was damned well going to find one. Enzo had saved him, dragged him from the depths, and given him new life. He would do anything to return the favor.

Enzo was worth fighting for.

A knock sounded upon the office door.

Enzo felt annoyance rise and gestured to Raymond to answer the door.

Sergei entered, expression grim, seating himself at a wave from Enzo, who was on the phone. Enzo listened intently, feeling tension rise, before hearing the words he had hoped for. He relaxed back into the leather chair. As if in concert, Raymond sighed, his body seeming to release its own tension. His aide had been party to the morning's dealings and had been making calls of his own.

For now, he enjoyed the last moments of talking to his friend. "*Sì*. Good to know, my friend. As always, if you need help, Santos, you only have to call. *Sì. Sì.* Good then. *Ciao.*" Enzo placed the phone down, swiveling to face Sergei fully.

"Well, you look like a bundle of joy, my friend. What are we dealing with now?"

Sergei sighed. "Paolo was killed about an hour ago on the west side of the city. He and two of his bodyguards were ambushed leaving a restaurant. Shot. All three died instantly."

Enzo stared at him for a long moment, then leaned back, fingers slowly curling over the front edge of the armrests. He felt a smile tugging at the corner of his lips. That was one less scheming uncle to contend with.

Sergei lifted his eyebrow. "There is something you are not telling me. You already knew, didn't you?"

"I have just been speaking with Santos. He said that he found moles in the southern lines, trying to create suspicion between us. They do not know how close we are or how often we communicate. He says that he did some investigating, forced some people to talk. The plot traced back to Paolo."

"So Santos ordered a hit on Paolo?" Sergei shook his head, confused.

It was unlike Santos to interfere on Enzo's domain, but Enzo could see how Sergei could jump to such a conclusion. "No. My guess is Benito."

"You knew that it was likely to be Paolo interfering in the south, so you offered Benito the leadership." Sergei was testing out the words slowly.

Enzo nodded. "I could hardly kill one of my own, Sergei. That would make me my father, wouldn't it?"

Sergei huffed out a laugh. "So you got Benito to turn on him. Slick." He leaned back in the chair, expression relaxing. "Still, I had thought them closer than that. I have to confess to being a little bit surprised."

"Honor among thieves? Come now, Sergei, have I not taught you better than that? Benito would kill his own son to become the Martinelli." Enzo curled his lip at the thought of father sacrificing son. Even his own father had never turned on Enzo, mad though he had been.

"So this way, they do the work for you, true to their nature. Are you not worried that Paolo's family will think this was you?" Raymond sounded skeptical.

"I simply put a bug in the right ear. The rumors lead back to Benito."

"You clever bugger." Sergei's laugh held admiration. "All without putting any of us in the line of fire."

"I do not waste wolves upon the elimination of mad dogs, my friend."

"This could get ugly damn quickly." Sergei's voice had a grim tone about it. "To pit Paolo's family against Benito's. It could tear the family apart."

Enzo said nothing. Didn't need to.

Sergei nodded. "You have no intention of preventing this war, do you? What are you up to, my friend?"

"For years I have stood at the head of this family, stepping in to keep things calm, preventing the bloodshed they long for so much. I am unwilling to continue to do so."

Sergei watched him in silence. Beside him, Raymond only nodded. Enzo was fully aware of what his aide thought of the Martinelli clan.

"You think I owe them loyalty?" Enzo's laugh sounded bitter to his own ears. "Do you forget what they did to my brother? They would have killed him in revenge for shooting our father. And yet, secretly they reveled in Father's demise, wanted his power, fought against my ascent to leadership. They used everything they could to topple me in the beginning, and it was only because of you and your men that I succeeded. The Martinellis are like a pack of feral dogs, just waiting for me to falter, to tear me down. I have spent most of my life protecting them, leading them, and now, I find myself resenting the waste."

"Because of Chase." Sergei's tone held nothing but approval.

Enzo felt a warmth in his chest at his friend's support.

"Chase wants more than I can give him at this moment. If it is at all possible, I want to be more for him. Better perhaps." Enzo tilted his lips with grim humor. "I don't really see how this will be possible, but…"

Sergei leaned forward, intensity in every line of his body.

"I am here, my friend. Whatever comes, I am here."

Raymond's hand on his shoulder seconded the statement.

Chase heard about the shooting later that day from Enzo, and he felt a chill run up his spine at the news. This could only lead to warfare amongst the family if Benito truly was the culprit.

Enzo seemed secure in that fact, and Chase could not understand his lack of response.

"Will you not have to look into this? Will they not blame you instead?" Concern for his lover was evident in his anxiety.

Enzo leaned forward to kiss him, where they sat at dinner in the huge banquet room of the house. The men and their significant others, whether male or female, came once a week to this room, where it was like a loud, noisy family. Chase loved it, loved the softness it brought to Enzo's expression. This was the family Enzo deserved, not those who sought his death in a quest for power.

"I have sent out some of my men to investigate, in clear sight. No one will be able to say I accepted this without action. Word on the street is already pointing to Benito though, as it did in your shooting."

Chase froze in place. "It was Benito who had me shot? Your own uncle? Why?" True bewilderment filled his expression, and Enzo reached out to stroke his cheek, loving the innocence that still remained within the boy, the lack of malice.

"Because he hates me. Because he and the family begrudge me the smallest amount of happiness. And you are my happiness."

The declaration fell straight to Chase's soul. He had never thought Enzo would voice his emotions so freely, and in front of others. He could not speak for the wonder he felt.

Enzo's lips quirked ever so slightly. "Do not ever think that I do not value you or treasure your presence. I am not good with flattery or fine words, but you are mine, Chase." His dark eyes flared with possessiveness, making Chase shiver with need.

In that moment, Chase knew that he had received his dearest wish. Enzo wanted him truly, needed him even. Surely there could be no greater joy in this lifetime.

Yet fear niggled at the edges of his consciousness. If the Martinellis began rending each other, Enzo would clearly be one of their targets. He clutched Enzo's hand more tightly and raised it to his lips, breathing a fervent prayer for protection over the tanned skin.

He caught Raymond's eye over Enzo's shoulder, and was surprised when the man nodded to him. The meaning was clear. Enzo would be protected at all costs.

Enzo strolled into the dining room, stooping to lay a kiss on Chase's lips as he passed.

Ms. Granger noted his arrival and bustled about the kitchen readying lunch for them.

"How is the paperwork going? Did you need help?" Enzo pulled a chair to Chase's side so he could view Chase's handiwork more closely.

Chase ran a hand through his ruffled hair once more, leaning to give Enzo a kiss of greeting.

"I think I'm finally done. Ms. Granger's youngest son went to college two years ago, so she remembers some of the paperwork and how to do it. It really helped. If the course is harder than these damned forms, I'm doomed."

Enzo tsk-tsked at him. "You are a smart and strong-minded young man. You will do fine. I cannot help but be pleased you chose the local college."

Chase snorted and looked at him askance. "As if I would leave you now? Please…" He rolled his eyes.

"The programs for architecture are more highly rated in Miami." Enzo thanked Ms. Granger as she set coffee before him.

"You are more important. It is going to be hard enough to leave you during the week, much less not even see you. This will be fine, and besides, I have Kirith. He can teach me more when we go there on holiday than any school ever could."

Enzo's lips tilted at mention of his younger brother. "He is a genius in the field, or so I have been told. I will have to tease some of that ego down, next time we go."

Chase signed the final paper, letting out a long sigh of relief. Shuffling them into a neat pile, he smiled as Ms. Granger placed breakfast in front of Enzo and then him. Reaching out, he pulled Ms. Granger in for a hug.

She swatted at him, flushed with pleasure, and disappeared

back into the environs of the kitchen.

Chase ate for several minutes with gusto, finding himself absolutely famished, musing silently on Enzo's words.

"When can we go see them? I miss them all, especially Kirith and Laura. And Landon, when he isn't teasing me unmercifully, can be a lot of fun."

Enzo growled ever so faintly, as he always did at mention of Landon's name.

"That boy is a menace."

Chase grinned, took a long drink of orange juice, and leaned in to give Enzo a citrus kiss. "You like him. You just don't want to."

Enzo refused to answer, focusing on the meal with rapt attention.

Chase laughed and nudged him. "Come on, admit it!"

Enzo scowled. "As long as he makes Kirith happy, I will tolerate him."

Chase rolled his eyes, bolting down his food. "I have to go take the forms in this afternoon and talk to the counselor there. I should be back by supper." Energy hummed through his veins, and he could scarcely stop himself from fidgeting. This was a big step in his life, something that would give him the independence he craved, while allowing him to remain at Enzo's side. With luck and perseverance, he hoped to create a career that would earn him Enzo's respect, and a way to stay home to be with his lover. If Kirith could do this, then so could he.

Enzo pulled him into a long kiss as he finished the meal, tongues winding about each other, sharing breath. It was hard to stand up afterward, and Chase could not resist bending down to capture another kiss. Enzo obliged, before giving him a smack upon the butt that made him yelp. Casting a reproachful glare at his lover, he rubbed his abused posterior.

"If I'm going to be abused, I'm not sure I want to rush back."

Enzo's eyes glinted. "I have paperwork and phone calls this

afternoon, but nothing after that. I thought we could spend time in the pool."

Chase's mind immediately supplied some rather vivid fantasies of exactly what they could get up to and how many positions.

He shook his head and stepped back. "Stop that. How am I supposed to focus on school when you put images like that in my mind?"

Enzo rose to his feet, and drew Chase to him with one arm, bending to kiss along his neck, before biting softly, leaving a reddened mark. "Mine," he growled. "Remember that, when you are there."

"As if I could forget," Chase replied somewhat breathlessly, leaning up for another kiss.

Enzo pulled back with a smile. "Go then. Think of cool water sliding along your skin."

Chase groaned, snatching up the papers and fleeing, Enzo's laughter making him smile.

Chapter Twelve

Enzo got off the phone to Santos with a feeling of satisfaction. His friend had definitely cleaned house, finding and removing a number of moles and tidying up several weak spots that had gone unnoticed. He had caught Santos up on events here and told him to keep an eye on Benito's work to see if he had the skill to head Enzo's southern connections.

He doubted it. With the Martinellis at each other's throats, sooner or later, his uncle's arrogance and bluster were going to get him killed, but it would not be by Enzo's hand. That his death was a forgone conclusion pleased him. He had harmed Chase. But simply to kill the man was not enough. For him to kill himself through stupidity, with the understanding that he had failed, that was enough revenge. For once, Enzo's hands would be clean.

The reason for his seeming patience was clear to him. To kill another in Chase's name would be distasteful and distressing to his lover. Therefore, it would be done more illusively, with the same result.

He could be patient.

He glanced outside at the sunshine trying to lure him onto the balcony, before sighing, and turning back to his desk. He had too much to do if he was going to devote the evening to Chase.

A knock on the door was welcome distraction from work.

"*Sì.*"

Raymond poked his head in, looking anything but pleased.

"Ren is here. Wanting to speak to you. Should I send him away?"

His eyebrow rose. Everything had seemed fine at their last meeting at the restaurant. Ren had been disappointed, yes, but hardly broken hearted. Whatever could he want so soon after their amiable split?

"Let him in. A friend should not be ignored."

Raymond expression tightened, but he nodded.

He sat back in his chair, stretching his back with a faint groan. Damn paperwork. It was one thing he would not miss if the family was to fall.

A faint knock on the doorframe made him look up.

Ren grinned at him and breezed into the room with his usual flair, sinking gracefully into the plush chair across from his desk.

"*Mio amico*! I was passing by and could not resist stopping in. I saw Rafael yesterday!"

Enzo relaxed. Nothing serious then — no play on trying to get back in his bed. He should have trusted Ren more. His friend had never played games with him, had always been to the point. He might be somewhat scattered, but he had been a true friend through the years, even if they had not remained in each other's pockets.

He smiled back, shaking his head.

"I have not seen Rafael in…ten years or so. What is the sneaky bastard up to?"

Ren gestured to the wine decanters on the sideboard. "Do you mind? I am parched. What can I get you?"

He sighed, looking at the amount of paperwork yet to be done. "Scotch. Neat. It might get me through this lot."

Ren chuckled as he rose, took his time selecting a wine, and poured it out before turning to Enzo's scotch.

"Rafael is the father of twins."

Enzo stared, before leaning back, and laughing out loud. "Rafael? Good God, I would love to see him trying to juggle two babies. Boys? Girls?"

"One of each, I was told." Ren finally turned back, a glass in each hand. He passed the scotch to Enzo and resumed his own seat, lounging back, and tasting the wine with an appreciative hum. He then held out the glass. "To our old friend and his new path of fatherhood."

Enzo picked up his glass and returned the gesture.

"To Rafael!"

He took a drink, the potent scotch sliding down his throat smoothly, though with a faint aftertaste that made him frown. He was sure he had already tasted some of this particular bottle, but…

"So how is your new relationship holding up? I was very sorry to hear about the shooting. I should have phoned you." Ren's voice was a little stiff, but Enzo was pleased he was making the effort to be polite about Chase.

"He is a tough one. Sergei whined about being shot the last time, much more than Chase did now." Enzo could not help but grin at the thought.

Ren arched an eyebrow, laughing. "Sergei? Whining? I find that hard to believe. The man is pure granite."

"He has his cracks, believe me!" He swirled his scotch, leaning his head back against the chair and watching Ren with a smile.

Ren shook his head ruefully. "I will have to take your word for it." He took another drink, savoring the fine wine. "So where is Chase anyway?"

"He is at the college today, handing in his forms and getting orientation." He could not help the proud expression.

Ren nodded. "I would have thought he would go to a larger college."

"He decided to stay here, at least in the short term."

"Couldn't leave you, hmm? Smart boy." There was the faintest bite in the words, and Enzo tilted his head to regard his friend more closely.

"We discussed this before, my friend. Yet now you seem…"

"Regretful? Damn right." Ren's voice held more bitterness than Enzo would have expected. "You have always been mine. It is hard to give that up."

He stared at him long moments, blinking. "We have never claimed each other. It was what made our friendship so solid. You would not have stood for possession any more than I would have. And we had spent a great deal of time apart before your return."

Ren looked down, clenching his jaw. "A great mistake. One I plan to correct."

He was puzzled by the intensity he was picking up from Ren. The man had always been moody and swift tempered, but this hard determination he was projecting was new. "It would please me greatly if we can keep our friendship intact. It is not as though I have that many close friends to squander. Time and circumstance have taken many of them from me."

He sighed silently, feeling weariness creep up upon him. With everything that was happening right now, he did not need another burden.

Ren attempted a stiff smile. "Forgive me. I am low today." He held out his glass again. "To our friendship and its continuation into old age."

Enzo picked up his scotch, smiling back. "To friendship." He took a stiff drink, needing something to give him strength. He had never been good at emotional speeches. When he went to set the glass down, his fingers shook and he almost spilled it, only Ren's quick action saving the precious scotch from waste.

Ren came around the desk, concern on his face. "You are pale, *mi amore*. Are you feeling well?"

He looked at his fingers with shock. They trembled noticeably, and he was beginning to feel faint. What in hell?

"You have been working too hard, as usual. Let's get you to the couch. Come." Ren drew him up from the chair, bracing him when he swayed alarmingly.

The couch seemed a million miles away, and he had never been so grateful to sink into the soft leather, laying down full length with a feeling of utter relief. His senses were swimming completely now, and when he tried to speak to Ren, only a hoarse croak emerged. His body was both hot and cold at the same time, and it was hard to think straight.

Ren stroked his hair back, intense eyes staring into his own. "Sleep, my friend. You will feel better when you wake."

Some instinct made Enzo fight against unconsciousness, no matter how it beckoned. Something was very, very wrong here. If he could just think…

The door opened, and Ren glanced up, relief in his expression. "You took your damned time. Did you get rid of his guards?"

"Done. Got Raymond to go downstairs. The helicopter will be here in ten."

Enzo's eyes widened at the familiar tone, disbelief beginning to get a foothold in his muddled senses.

No. This could not be happening.

"Help me carry him. Then you can do your worst." Ren's voice held cold malice. "Especially to the kid."

Enzo half sat up, adrenaline clearing the weakness for a precious moment, disbelief fading into fury.

Ren turned to him, easily blocking the movement, effortlessly forcing Enzo back down onto the couch. He leaned in, a look of smug satisfaction and triumph written across his face.

"You are mine. Always have been. No kid is going to take that away from me." He leaned in, traced his fingers over Enzo's cheek, his eyes filled with honest emotion. "I have saved you, my love. They would have killed you, but I brokered a deal for us. By the time we reach our destination, it will all be over, and we can start anew, free of the family. You don't understand right now, but…"

The shot was quiet enough, silenced down to a faint pop, but the effect was no less horrific. Ren's head virtually disappeared, and Enzo gagged as blood and other matter sprayed his face. Ren's lifeless body slumped to the floor in front of the couch, and Enzo managed to look up, meeting familiar eyes.

No.

"Stupid fucker. Actually thought we would let you go. But it was great he drugged you. Helped a lot." The smile was cold and malicious. "But now you die. Not fast, not like him. The house is rigged to blow as soon as I leave. Not right here, just close enough to start a massive fire."

He turned away, paused in the doorway to look back.

"Goodbye, *Enzo*." He savored the name. "You have made me a very rich man with your death." A light laugh, and he was gone.

Enzo struggled to sit, fury and betrayal giving him momentary strength.

He managed to get mostly vertical, panting. He tried to call out, but his voice was faint, wavering. Cursing weakly, he tried to push himself forward, get his legs under him, crawl if he had to. Where the fuck was everyone? Fear for their fate gave him fresh impetus, and he slid to the floor, forcing himself past the drugs.

The move saved his life. The blast was enormous, blowing out the west wall of the office, and throwing the massive bookshelf there halfway across the room, striking the back of the heavy couch, and pushing it forward with abrupt and painful force. Books rained down upon Enzo, half stunning him, and in the aftermath, he could only lay there, now pressed up against Ren's body in a macabre imitation of their lovemaking.

He could hear flames now, licking softly at first, then gaining force, heat swirling over him.

Even turning his head took an effort of mammoth proportions, and his gaze fell upon the half-open door, beckoning.

There was no more strength to be had. His fingers clenched upon Ren's silk shirt as he felt the first lick of flame upon his body, biting back a silent scream.

He whispered a prayer of thankfulness as the drugs took him first, and he faded into darkness, his last thoughts of his lover and what they could have had.

Chase hummed as he drove, fingers keeping a beat on the steering wheel as his radio blared. The orientation had gone well, and the people he would share the class with seemed interesting and pleasant enough. He was eager to start and could not help but laugh at himself. Before, college had seemed like a fateful chore, destined to take him from Enzo. Now... Now it held the key to his future beside his lover, not a burden but a true partner.

He turned into the street that led toward home, frowning as he noticed the number of cars and people. Newspeople...

His heart began to pound in a strange irregular rhythm as he came up the last hill, out of the trees, and saw Tanglewood spread before him, smoke filling the sky.

Flames.

The villa, the vast buildings — engulfed.

He slammed to a stop in the middle of the street, unable to go further past emergency vehicles and people. Wrenching the car door open, ignoring the stares of the gawkers, he flew down the street, pushing his way past people, uncaring of their curses.

His breath was caught in his chest, tight and immovable, a sob rising to his throat.

Police guarded the entranceway at the great stone gates, and one turned, reaching out to grab Chase.

He ducked and rolled over the hood of the nearest police car, uncaring of the shouts behind him. His feet pounded the concrete driveway. He could feel the heat now, rolling toward him, the fire trucks and their crews seeming to make no impact upon the inferno.

Up ahead, seated dejectedly upon the lawn in the huge circular driveway, sat several of Enzo's men, blackened with soot. Medics knelt before some, treating burns.

Chase stopped abruptly, staring, then stumbled toward them, his gaze frantically searching.

One of the figures looked up as he approached, then stood on shaking legs to greet him.

Chase grabbed Rafe's shirtfront, breathless, frantic.

"What the fuck happened? Where—"

Something in the bodyguard's red-rimmed eyes made Chase take a step back.

No. Dear God. No.

Rafe reached toward him, gently taking his hand.

"Where is Enzo?" Chase's body began to shake uncontrollably, his fingers clenching upon Rafe's black-smeared hand.

Rafe could not even speak. He just shook his head, his whole posture one of defeat.

Chase stared at him, swallowing hard, then glanced around again desperately.

"Where's Sergei? Sergei will have Enzo. He would never let him get hurt. Right? Where is he? Where's Raymond?" His voice was rising.

"We're the only ones who got out of the main building," Rafe whispered hoarsely. "We were in the west wing when the blast happened, otherwise we would have been in there." He gestured to the flames, before shuddering and turning away. "The staff got out before the fire started in their area. Raymond was somewhere in between. He survived, but he is in bad shape. They don't know if he will make it, they rushed him to hospital."

"Blast? An explosion? From what?" Chase could not believe

this was happening. It could not happen, not here, not to Enzo.

"We've been trying to figure it out," Rafe murmured, holding Chase's hand gently in his. "We think it might be a murder-suicide."

Chase stared at him in shock. "Why…"

"Just shortly before the blast, Ren arrived here, and Enzo let him into his office. That bastard was crazy to begin with. I could see him doing something like this."

Chase slid down to his knees, tears rising. He had warned Enzo about Ren. That the man would not give up his prize so easily. Never had he thought of this, and obviously, neither had Enzo.

Enzo…

A sob rose, and he leaned into Rafe as the bodyguard slid down beside him. Suddenly, feverishly, he dug in his pocket and pulled out his phone. He needed help, he needed support. There was only one person who could make this right. Enzo could not be dead.

He pressed the speed dial.

"Hello?' The deep voice was comfort itself.

"Kirith…"

Chase sat in the gathering darkness, oblivious of the ash that rained softly down upon his numb form. His arms were wrapped around his knees, and he rocked, ever so slightly, his mind blank. Rafe and the others stayed clustered protectively around him, some of them with tear tracks upon blackened faces.

The police had warned them they would be coming to the nearest station for questioning on the fire, but they were also noticeably nervous about forcing them. The seven bodyguards left were imposing enough to warrant caution.

The sound of the helicopter was almost lost amid the constant roaring hiss, as the firefighters struggled against the inferno, water making little impression.

Chase turned his head slowly, as he saw the police shifting rifles, nervously eyeing the eight newcomers.

The man who led them ignored the police presence entirely, striding forward, long pale hair gleaming in the shifting firelight. Chase felt his heart break as he saw the horror upon Kirith's face as he viewed the remnants of his brother's beloved home.

Stiffly rising, he forced his legs into motion, and moments later found himself enfolded in strong arms. He sobbed then, broken, shaking uncontrollably.

Another voice murmured soothingly, then he was hugged from behind, safely ensconced between Kirith and Landon.

"I've got you, Chase," Kirith whispered, kissing the top of his head. "You are never alone. You are part of my family, now and always."

Chase squeezed his eyes shut and nestled closer against that hard chest, burying himself, never wanting to face the world again.

Kirith guided Chase out of the police station with a warm hand low on his back, protective.

The boy was in pieces, and the questioning had not helped the matter. Kirith had barely managed to keep his mouth shut during the procedure and had coldly refused to speak of his missing brother when they had turned the questions upon him.

They had been told that Chase couldn't leave the area until the investigation was complete. This presented a problem in that Kirith couldn't take him back to the island, as he had planned. They would have to remain here, and here was a dangerous place for Kirith. The sharks that made up the Martinelli family would be only too glad finally to see him dead. Killing his father had made him a target, and only Enzo's intervention and his exile to the Caribbean had saved him. To be here, now, amid such uncertainty, was suicidal.

Landon was a nervous wreck, having called in more men and surrounding Kirith and Chase with guards.

Kirith didn't protest as he usually did. Now wasn't the time for personal freedoms.

Enzo's seven bodyguards were waiting outside, having gone through their own questioning, and Landon hurried everyone into waiting vans, unwilling to have his lover and Chase exposed.

Sitting with his arm around Chase's shoulders, feeling the young man lean into him, Kirith tried to stay positive. Enzo was not an easy man to kill. There was still hope. His brother couldn't be dead.

He stared out the window, his chest tight with emotion.

Enzo couldn't be dead. Please, dear God, I beg you.

Chase approached the hospital bed with caution, eyes filling with tears he could not withhold.

Raymond lay unconscious, hooked up to machines, his battered face looking like nothing familiar.

He had always been wary of this man, despite the fact he had never tried to harm Chase in any way, shape or form.

Now, he was the only one left of the triad, of the unbreakable friendship of Enzo, Sergei, and Raymond.

He reached out, laid a tentative hand over Raymond's arm, in a small area that did not seem to have bruises and contusions.

"We're with you, Raymond. Don't you give up, all right? We need you." His voice choked off. "Enzo will need you when we find him. We *will* find him. I know it. We have to. And Sergei, he will be OK too. He will. You just need to get better and it will all be fine. Please." His voice failed him.

He turned away into Kirith's broad chest, breaking down finally into uncontrollable sobs.

Chapter Thirteen

"You need to eat."

Chase looked up, taking some moments to identify the speaker.

Rafe attempted a smile, though it was shaky at best. "I made some toast. Thought you might like a piece."

Chase just stared at him, unable to take in the words.

Rafe pushed a plate of buttered toast toward him. "We have to keep going. Enzo would not want you to grieve yourself into illness."

Chase felt the tears rise again, and he ducked his head, staring blindly at the offered toast. Tentatively, he reached out and took a piece, biting into it listlessly.

He choked it down and was rewarded with Rafe's relieved smile. "I've got to look after you. Enzo would expect that of me and the others. You have to let me do my job. It's all I have left." He looked away then, and Chase roused himself enough to lay a comforting hand on his arm.

Rafe took several deep breaths and turned back, putting his own hand over Chase's. "When this is all over, you need to go to college, just like you had planned."

Chase stared at him in disbelief. "I'll go back to the island. I want to be with Kirith." He rubbed his tear-swollen eyes. "I can't stay here."

"You can. Do you think Enzo would have wanted you to quit? After how hard you have worked for this?"

Chase curled into the kitchen chair, wrapping his arms around his torso in a futile search for comfort.

"Look, I've got a fairly large house, and I have already taken in two of the other guys who lived here. There's an extra bedroom, and it is just two blocks from the college. You could even walk there. You have to have something to do, Chase. You'll go crazy otherwise. He wanted this for you. Don't let him down now. Plus you can visit Raymond. The doctors seem to think there is hope he'll pull through, and maybe with you there…"

Chase bit his lip against further tears. He had done nothing but cry for the whole week since the fire.

No miracle had saved his heart. There was no sign of Enzo. Kirith's men were searching, but so far, nothing. It was becoming clear that Enzo had indeed been in that house and had not made it out.

Chase's world had ended. He could not sleep, could not eat or think.

Rafe's words impacted his mind with startling force. He could not, would not let Enzo down. That was what he had always sworn and had worked so diligently toward. But to go to classes, as if nothing had happened, as though he was not shattered and broken. But, for Raymond, to be there for someone Enzo had cared for so much…

"I'll think about it," he whispered finally, feeling Rafe's hand rub comfortingly over his back. "Thank you."

Rafe smiled, small and tentative. "We're all that's left. We have to stick together, you know?"

Chase nodded, but his heart felt cold, and he wondered with dim desperation how he could possibly go forward.

Kirith sat in the shade of the patio, sipping coffee and watching Chase and Rafe walk down by the ornate fountains of the rented house. It was good the boy had a friend in the bodyguard. He was so alone now, so fragile.

He heard footsteps and leaned back in his chair as Landon bent over and kissed him lightly before sinking into a chair beside him.

Kirith gestured for more coffee to be brought and eyed his lover questioningly, hoping…

"Nothing," Landon grunted, looking tired and fed up. "Not a goddamned thing." He leaned forward and took Kirith's hand. "It's not looking good, Kir. I hate to say it, but if our team has found nothing…"

Kirith felt his chest tighten, and he bit his lip viciously to prevent tears from rising. Chase needed him to be strong right now, not to fall to pieces.

His Enzo—his beloved brother. He had always feared that this would happen. Enzo lived far too violent a life for this not to be a possibility, but to die so needlessly at the hands of a friend…

He drew in a deep shuddering breath, trying to control himself, unable to meet Landon's concerned gaze. How was he going to tell Laura that her much loved *zio* was gone? Kirith scrubbed a hand over his face, feeling the shake in his hand. This was all so unbelievable. There seemed to be nothing in him that could accept that Enzo was dead. His brother was so strong, so dynamic and powerful, that death itself seemed unable to touch him.

And yet, now, it seemed it had suddenly and viciously ripped him away from them.

Enzo was not the only one lost either. As far as they could tell, at least six of the men on duty that day had died in the explosion and resulting inferno as well, including Sergei.

Thoughts of the grim captain made Kirith squeeze his eyes shut in a paroxysm of further grief. He had always liked the man who had been Enzo's shadow, and later his best friend and guardian.

Sergei had been kind to a younger brother, his grim features always softening in Kirith's presence. Whatever had happened, he would not have gone down quietly and not without being at Enzo's side.

His mind shied from the images of being trapped in that god-awful fire. He prayed fervently that all concerned had been dead or unconscious, that they never suffered. He was unable to sleep for the thought of that suffering. Landon had had to soothe him from recurring nightmares ever since.

He wanted to go to the hospital that evening, touch Raymond, make sure the man was still there, still alive. Kirith had never feared Raymond, had always trailed around after him when he was younger and the man's patience had shown a completely different side to his character.

Now, Kirith could give back, if only Raymond would wake up.

Landon pulled his chair closer and wrapped his arms around Kirith, who dimly realized that he was shivering uncontrollably at the direction of his thoughts.

Despite his partner's comforting presence, he suddenly felt very alone, without the shelter of his brother's unconditional love. The foundation of their lives had suddenly been torn away, and everything teetered precariously at its loss.

Chase was speechless.

"You are a very wealthy young man now," Ray Stein intoned gravely, shuffling papers, as he finally looked up into Chase's stunned face.

The lawyer then glanced at Kirith, who was struggling to withhold emotion at this blatant reminder of his brother's love. "As are you, Mr. Martinelli. Neither of you will ever want for anything. Your brother invested shrewdly, and with caution, and there is absolutely nothing to link any of this with his other — dealings. This is all above board and scrupulously clean. Nobody else can touch it. As well as the businesses, there are several homes involved in different parts of the country and a large isolated ranch in Canada."

"A ranch?" Chase whispered in disbelief, that fact above others seeming unreal to him.

Ray cleared his throat, and sat back in his chair, regarding them both with sad eyes. "I was under the impression from what Enzo told me, that he had some designs of retiring there permanently."

Chase shook his head, glancing at Kirith for support. "I can't imagine Enzo wanting to be anywhere near a ranch. He didn't seem to be the kind to enjoy that lifestyle."

Kirith gave a weary smile, edged with grief. "He loved horses. Had from the time he was little apparently, even took some riding lessons when he was younger. When he was training as an assassin down in South America, they did a lot of travelling on horseback through regions that vehicles cannot possibly reach, and I know he loved it."

Chase felt a pang in his chest. He had known nothing of this. Enzo had never mentioned it to him, and it brought about the realization that he knew so little of the man who had been his lover.

Had been.

Tears rose again. He felt that he should have run dry a long time ago, but still the sorrow did not cease. Would never cease. How could he ever move past this loss? Impossible. There was no one in the world like Enzo. No one could possibly ever take Enzo's place in his heart.

He glanced over at Kirith's wan and exhausted features. Nor in Kirith's either.

A month now, and the pain was an ever present ache for the two of them.

They left the lawyer's office in stunned silence, Landon guiding both Kirith and Chase through the waiting bodyguards and into the car.

Chase stared out the window, silent despair overwhelming him as he realized how little he knew of his lover. They had had so short a time, just beginning their journey together, just starting to learn each other's secrets.

Now, it had ended.

He sagged against the leather seat, cold reality washing over him. A month had passed. Landon's team had found nothing.

Enzo was dead.

His heart could not accept that. Foolish though it was, there was still a sliver of hope in his heart. Kirith was the same. Perhaps only time itself would cure them of such madness and make them see the cold truth.

Perhaps time would ease this unbearable sense of emptiness as well.

They arrived back at the rented house in weary silence. Landon hustled them in the door, uneasy with them being outside at all.

"Daddy!" Laura sprang up from the deep leather couch, flinging herself upon her father.

Chase watched Kirith's expression lighten as he embraced his daughter with fervent appreciation. With the extended stay here, they had had no choice but to bring Laura from the safety of the island to this well-guarded house.

She clung to him, giving him kisses and stroking his face anxiously. Laura, though she grieved for her *zio* deeply, had found comfort in caring for them all, fussing over them, and giving love freely and often. She seemed so mature in her manner, so unlike a ten-year-old. Yet her experiences of the past, kidnapped alongside her father, had changed her radically. Her eyes were too old for a child, her thoughts above and beyond her age. To put aside her own loss in favor of helping others…

She would grow up to be an amazing woman, Chase mused, managing a smile as she turned to him. Her hug and kiss was cathartic, and he drank in her love with gratitude. She left his side to go to Landon, and Chase saw the love they held for each other.

For just a moment, Landon's stoic mask cracked, and he saw the stress the other man was under, trying so desperately to keep Kirith, Chase, and Laura safe, and comfort his devastated lover.

They were all falling to pieces, and Chase saw no way to halt the process. Perhaps time itself, but that was vague and far away, the pain too present and sharp.

The only good news was that Raymond had regained consciousness at last. His memory was sketchy at best, and there was no guarantee of what would return, but he was improving day by day.

Kirith was already making plans to move him to the island for rehabilitation, once the rest of them could return.

They ate supper together, Laura chivying both Kirith and Chase to eat. Both had been losing weight, and Chase found himself complying, more to inspire Kirith than to satisfy himself.

Kirith could not afford to go back into the old patterns he had fallen into after his kidnapping. It had taken all this time for him to gain back his muscle mass and proper fitness. For him, Chase choked down the tasteless food, though he felt ill afterward.

They clustered in the living room, gathering to watch one of Laura's favorite movies. Laura snuggled up to her father on the right, with Chase on Kirith's left, sandwiched comfortingly between Kirith and Landon. Both men held him close, and he leaned his head on Landon's shoulder, drinking in the warmth of body and mind. They genuinely cared about him, were not going to abandon him. It seemed so unreal.

If only there was not a void within them all.

Somebody was missing.

Kirith watched Chase's despondent figure disappear into the doors of the college and slumped against the back seat of the car, letting out a sigh of both relief and frustration. It had taken every bit of persuasion to get Chase to this point, and he was utterly worn out.

This was Chase's future. He needed this desperately, but all his personal strength had been geared toward pleasing Enzo. Now, it seemed, he had nothing to inspire him, and it had taken long, hard work to get him to the point he could do this.

Landon slid closer, wrapping his arm around him in comfort. "We'll get him through this. Once he meets new people, gets involved, it will help."

Kirith leaned into the loving touch, soaking up his lover's vitality and strength. For so many years, he had longed to leave the island, be able to see the mainland again and all its diversity. Now that he was here, he wanted nothing more than to return to the peace and tranquility of his home. Only now did he realize how precious such a thing truly was. He had never truly been a part of Enzo's world, and now he had proof that it was nothing he wanted and never would.

The threat of the family hung over them at all times, and the silence on the part of Benito was nerve-wracking, to say the least. He had made no attempt to contact them, no sign of upholding the exile that had kept Kirith upon the island. No word or sign of how he perceived Enzo's death.

Benito was the Martinelli now, as he had striven for.

Kirith could not imagine he would be merciful. The very silence was intimidating. Landon had the entire team here now, including their leader, Captain Brian Forenza. Kirith felt better with his presence. His fear was not for himself, but for his precious daughter. Laura had gone through too much already. He never wanted another hint of violence to mar her life again after what she had already been through on his behalf.

He shuddered at the memories, staring out the window blindly, as the car negotiated the busy streets.

Wrenching his thoughts away took effort, but he refused to return to that dark place. He had come too far and worked far too hard to regress now.

Soon, once Chase had settled at school, Kirith could return to the island. Chase had decided to move into Rafe's house with the other guards. It was probably the safest place he could possibly be right now.

He would miss Chase, but he could not continue to endanger Laura by keeping her here within reach of the family. Who knew what the new Martinelli regime may want with her?

Chase could visit the island during school breaks, and hopefully that would be enough to keep him connected with his adopted family. Kirith worried that Chase would slip into depression, that school would not be enough to take his thoughts from Enzo even a little.

He closed his eyes as thoughts came round again to his brother. To die in such a manner...

He could only hope the explosion had killed them all before the fire ever started. He had received the initial police reports yesterday, showing the size and probable placement of the bomb and the terrible force it would have unleashed. He shuddered, then suddenly froze, a realization coming to the fore.

He leaned forward, tapping the shoulder of the bodyguard in the passenger seat. Tony turned his head, his own features tired and worn. He was one of the survivors of the blast, and he had lost many friends that day.

"Tony, when Ren entered the house that day, was he carrying anything?"

The bodyguard blinked, then frowned in thought. "No." His eyes widened as he realized where Kirith's thoughts were travelling. "He had nothing. He could not have concealed a bomb with that much power."

Kirith felt a chill feather down his spine.

Whatever had happened in that office, Ren was not the bomber.

Chapter Fourteen

Chase felt like he had been wrung out and left to dry. He was grateful that he had only had two classes for this first day. It was now noon, and he had nothing left, his mind churning, his body limp with exhaustion. He could not wait to get home. He swallowed hard, sucking in a quivering breath.

There was no *home* anymore.

There was no place that was familiar and welcoming, that contained the man he loved.

There was nothing.

He shook his head with a surge of anger. That wasn't true. Ren hadn't taken everything from him. He had a family that wouldn't abandon him this time. He had Kirith, Landon, and Laura. He had the tattered remnants of Enzo's men, who had rallied round him. Raymond, if he recovered. And Rafe, who'd encouraged him to stay at college. He wasn't alone. He was still part of the family, scattered and broken as it may be.

Even if his heart was frozen, there were those who loved him.

He groaned with heartfelt despair when he exited the building and saw Rafe waiting for him with a small smile. He had promised to go shopping today, to start to get his furnishings for his new life in Rafe's house. There was nothing he wanted to do less at this moment. He was grateful to his friend for the offer of room and board, but at this moment, he did not have the resources even to care. He had considered getting his own place — after all he could well afford it now thanks to Enzo's investments — but he feared being alone. He knew all too well the dark places in his soul, and he had no wish to return to them. To be alone would be to live with Enzo's ghost, and he would never survive the memories if he did not have someone to snap him out of it.

Rafe reached out and snagged his backpack, swinging it into the back of the rental car with swift efficiency. Chase felt a twinge of annoyance at the fact that he had half bowed under its weight, but the bodyguard found its mass negligible. He was going to have to work out more, eat more. Sometimes he felt more than a little insignificant next to his new housemates.

Still, Enzo had chosen him. Just the way he was. He had to remember that.

He held that thought tightly, holding his lover's memory close. It was the only comfort he had now.

He slid into the car and slumped in the seat, wondering wearily how long it would take before the searing pain of loss became something he could live with.

Rafe drew him close for a hug, then kissed his temple. Chase drew back, shooting a glance at his friend. Rafe shrugged, then started the car.

"You looked like you needed it."

Chase relaxed, chiding himself for being jittery. It had been the gesture of a friend, no more. Yet sometimes, he felt more from Rafe than he was ready to accept. Their past, and Rafe's admiration, loomed over them both, and Chase was not prepared to let anything get out of hand.

In the future...maybe. He could not envision the future right now. Maybe in time, Rafe's feelings could be returned, but right now there was only Enzo. The mere thought of another man touching him in passion was completely repugnant. Rafe seemed to understand, but if that changed, Chase would have to find another place to live.

The furniture store was vast, and Chase dithered, unable to bring his mind to bear upon the task at hand. He had managed to pick out a dresser, and a night table, but he couldn't bear to look at the beds yet. It seemed like an acceptance of fate, of Enzo's death, to have another bed of his own.

Rafe patiently followed, making notes of the stock numbers, his hand always upon Chase—a shoulder, the small of his back, sometimes cradling the nape of his neck in comfort—while Chase struggled to keep his shit together.

Chase's cell rang, and he pulled it out of his pocket with a sigh of relief. He was more than ready to take a break.

Need you home. Will go out to supper. Please soon. — K.

Chase frowned and put the phone away, grabbing Rafe's arm and heading for the doors. "Kirith wants me back."

Rafe protested, "What about the furniture?"

"I can get it later. You have the numbers. I can't face choosing a bed today anyway. Kirith needs me now."

Rafe frowned as they exited the building. "He demands too much of you. It will be good when he goes back to the island, and you can have a life."

Chase stood beside the car, staring at him in disbelief. "Kirith is my family. I will always be ready to help him, to go to him. Don't think that is going to change."

Rafe scowled for a moment, then opened the driver's door, remotely unlocking Chase's side.

Chase slid in, feeling a spike of anxiety shiver down his spine. That brief sense of hostility on Rafe's part seemed counter to everything the bodyguard had shown him so far in the way of friendship. How could he even imagine that Chase would be glad to see Kirith go? There was a hint of possessiveness there, something Chase wouldn't accept or endure in a friend. This was what he had been worried about.

Something else to face. He'd have to make it perfectly clear to Rafe that such a thing was unacceptable. He had thought he had been very succinct in his expectations of Rafe's friendship, making it plain that there was a line that could not be crossed, but now...

He stared out the window as they headed back to the rented house in silence.

Chase sighed to himself.

He was relieved when they finally entered the gates of the rented estate, the house looming before them.

He exited the car with a feeling of relief, feeling a certain amount of exasperation as Rafe dogged his heels into the house. When it seemed his companion would follow him upstairs to the family's rooms, he stopped abruptly and turned to face the bodyguard.

"I'm fine, Rafe. I need to talk to Kirith, and then we are probably all going out for supper. OK?"

Rafe stared at him, something foreign in his expression, before he gave a smile, erasing the image back to his usual mellow self. "OK. Sounds good. Give me a call if you need anything."

Chase rolled his eyes, patting Rafe's shoulder. "Yes, Mother. Talking of having to get a life, you need to relax a bit."

Rafe shook his head. "I lost a lot of friends, Chase. I have to protect you in Enzo's name. I can't lose anyone else."

Chase melted, sympathy overwhelming his caution. He gave his friend a hug, Rafe's arms enclosing him completely. He felt a warmth grow, chasing away the cold for a brief moment. Rafe was so giving, so patient. Chase finally stepped back and gave a tentative smile.

"I am fine. Nothing to worry about."

Rafe nodded, but there was nothing of acceptance in his

expression.

Chase sighed, turning to go up the staircase. Halfway up, a movement at the top of the stairs caught his attention, and he smiled up at Kirith, who had appeared on the landing. The grimness of Kirith's features caught Chase's attention, and he hurried the last few stairs. He heard sudden running steps behind him, shouts from below, and he started to turn, saw Rafe reaching for him, watching in shock as Kirith withdrew a gun from behind his waist and shot, cool and calm, nothing but ice in his expression.

Chase whirled on the spot, almost falling down the stairs, only Kirith's sudden grip saving him.

Rafe lay halfway up the stairs behind him, holding his shoulder, bodyguards swirling over him, pulling a gun from his hand.

He held out his good hand to Chase, a pleading expression upon his features, and Chase tugged against Kirith's hold, horrified, wanting to go to him. He was hurt…

"Don't, Chase. It was him. He planted the bomb." Kirith's voice was utterly steady, the rage of the words hidden deeply beneath control.

Chase froze, staring down at Rafe. He wanted to disbelieve, but in that moment, something in his friend's eyes, the lack of protest at being shot, it all made sense in a horrible, twisted kind of way.

He turned away, slumping into Kirith's strong arms. This betrayal was the last and worst.

Kirith and Chase sat in silence upon one of the leather couches, watching the sun set through the massive west windows.

Chase huddled under Kirith's arm, curled into him, clenching Kirith's shirt in his fingers.

Somewhere else in the city, Rafe was being questioned by Brian's team, including Landon, along with Enzo's bodyguards. It was a given he would not live long.

Chase had wept earlier, but now he was silent, perhaps too numb to vocalize his pain any further.

Kirith rubbed his back in slow, comforting circles and listened to Chase's unsteady breathing, wishing he could give more than the warmth of his body for solace.

They had not said anything for over an hour now. They were waiting. Waiting for news, for some explanation of how and why this had happened. Landon had been furious that none of them had suspected earlier that the killer had been amongst them, close to Kirith and Chase all the while.

Chase shivered, and Kirith made a soothing sound in his throat, drawing him closer, and laying a kiss on the top of his head.

There was a knock on the doorframe that led into the living room, and Kirith turned his head slowly and wearily to face Tony and beckon him forward.

"Sorry to disturb you, sir. But we just got some news about the family you might be interested in."

Kirith nodded.

"We got word, sir, that there seems to be some sort of turf war going on between Benito's men and Paolo's men. Seems Paolo's death created a lot of resentment, and it exploded last night, literally. Benito's house was destroyed, although he and his family were not there, and now, apparently, they are hunting each other down, the whole family getting pulled into it. I think, sir, that perhaps the absence of your brother has taken away all restraint."

Kirith felt a faint surge of vicious pleasure. The family had never been kind to him, always making sure he knew he was an outsider. As far as he was concerned, they were feral beasts, only Enzo's strength keeping them from rending each other to pieces.

Without a strong leader, they had reverted to form, and although he felt for the wives and children who would be caught up in the furor, he could not say he was sorry for what the outcome of this would be. The fall of the Martinellis gave him no grief whatsoever.

There were other groups, waiting in the wings, that would gladly take over, sensing weakness. This demonstration of turmoil within was tantamount to suicide in their line of work.

"Thank you, Tony," Kirith murmured. "Keep me apprised of any more news."

"Yes, sir. Should I send in food? It's getting late, and neither of you have eaten today."

Kirith managed a faint smile in acknowledgement of the bodyguard's concern.

"That's a good idea. Something simple though. A sandwich maybe."

Tony nodded, his brisk steps echoing down the hallway as he left.

"Are you all right?" Chase straightened up from his curled position, eyeing Kirith carefully. "These are your relations."

Kirith made a derisive sound, stroking Chase's rumpled hair back. "My mother was my family. Enzo was my family. Laura, Landon, and you are my family now. I hold no ties to the others."

"Thank you." Chase flushed.

Kirith managed a smile. "You did not give me a lot of choice. Wormed your way right in. Can't get rid of you now."

Chase elbowed him, earning a grunt.

"I want to go back to the island with you. I can't go back to school. Not now, not for a while. Maybe I can take some initial online courses, and you can give me tips. I just want to be away from here, away from people. I need time to grieve. I need all of you around me. Is that being weak?" He glanced at Kirith with some trepidation. "I can help with Raymond. I helped you before."

Kirith leaned forward and kissed his forehead, cupping his cheek gently in one hand. "I think you are wise enough to know your own mind and what you need. You have had a lifetime of other people forcing you into molds you did not want and then later guiding you for your own good. Now you are your own man, and I will respect whatever you feel you need." He rose to his feet and stretched. "You need to trust yourself. I do. As for Raymond, I can think of no one better to aid in his recovery. You give others strength."

He smiled down at Chase. "I am going to go wake Laura up, so she can eat with us. Her presence might make the two of us actually consume something."

Chase reached out and grasped Kirith's right hand, bringing it to his lips and kissing the back. "Thank you," he whispered. "You are always there for me."

"You are easy to love, Chase. Don't forget, you were there for me when I needed you. This is no one-way street. You are a strong, intelligent young man, and I am proud to be here for your journey."

Chase's eyes welled with tears. Kirith's thumb gently swept them away. "No more tears. Enzo would have scoffed at us, being so emotional. Time to be thankful for what we have, not what we have lost. Our grief will not go away, not so soon, but perhaps we can think of what we loved about him, and not so much about his death."

Chase nodded, but Kirith could see there was no belief in his thoughts.

They forced themselves to eat, Laura urging them on before she went back to her room to draw pictures for them both. Kirith turned on the TV, he and Chase watching the shows with blind apathy. The sound of footsteps approaching lent a welcome respite.

Landon stepped into the room. In a moment, Kirith was up and had his arms around him, guiding him to sit upon the couch, Chase on one side, Kirith on the other.

Kirith's lover was pale and haunted looking, and he gripped Kirith's hand with almost crushing force. He refused to meet his lover's eyes.

"This is my fault," he whispered, the words almost torn from him.

Kirith reached out to turn his face gently, so he had to meet his gaze. "What nonsense is this, my love?"

Landon stared at him for a long moment, then tried to pull away.

"It was Adrian who set this up. My brother. My own goddamned brother."

Kirith froze. "I thought he was dead. I thought Marcello killed him."

Landon gave a choked laugh, a note of hysteria in it. "No such luck. The bastard slipped out of it, somehow, the way he always has. He has been maneuvering, all this time, trying to get payback." His hand shook in Kirith's grip. "He blames me for our family's mercenary team collapsing. He has a lot of money set aside, and he paid Rafe, set the whole thing up. He provided the bomb. The clever bastard found the chinks in our armor, found Rafe, found Ren." He looked at Kirith with tears rising in his eyes. "This is my fault. Enzo died because of my family. Sergei and the others. Raymond injured. Oh God, my love, I am so sorry."

Kirith gathered him fully into his arms as Landon broke down completely.

"This is *not* your fault in any way, shape, or form, my love. You cannot control the actions of others. There was no way to know that Adrian still lived, no way to predict this atrocity. It is fully possible that Ren would have done this on his own or that Rafe would have taken action to try to possess Chase without outside influence. You cannot blame yourself for this. Just because you are related to the bastard does not mean you are implicated or should hold blame. Should I take responsibility for any of the horrors my family have perpetrated over the years?"

Landon jerked up, pulled Kirith forward for a frantic kiss. "No. Don't you ever compare yourself to them."

"Then don't take on your brother's behavior. This is none of your doing."

Landon buried his head against Kirith's shoulder. "I hate the bastard. I don't care we share blood."

Kirith stroked his lover's hair back with gentle fingers. "He and Nate tortured you as you grew up, kept you as a virtual prisoner under their thumb. I am not surprised you hold no brotherly sentiments toward him."

"Brian has men out searching for him already. I couldn't bring myself to…join them." His voice broke with emotion.

"I should think not." Kirith was horrified at the very notion. Adrian would meet his comeuppance, but it would not be at Landon's hands. His lover would never be able to wash the blood from his conscience if he took part in such a thing.

"This is for others to deal with, Landon. Your brothers have made your life a misery for so long. Don't let them bring you grief now. This is nothing of your doing. There is nothing in my heart that feels even the slightest hint of blame toward you. Don't let this bring you grief or bring a shadow between us that does not need to exist."

Chase hugged Landon from the other side, pressing him between them, shielding him.

Kirith put his arm around them both, feeling Landon's tears against his shoulder. These two men held his heart. One as a younger brother, one as his beloved partner. No matter what else had happened, the three of them would get through.

It was time to return to the island.

Chapter Fifteen

K irith and Chase sat in the shade of the palm trees, going over Chase's lessons, blond and silver heads bent close together as they worked.

Kirith reveled in the feel of the sun, in the sense of "home," as he pressed close to Chase's side. He had loved the island before, but always with an edge of nostalgia for the mainland.

He had been virtually imprisoned here far before Landon's arrival.

Now, it seemed a protective haven. His lover by his side, Chase safe at last. Raymond being cared for at the house.

Still, they did not relax their guard. A large portion of Brian's forces, Landon's teammates, were here in full protective mode. No chances were being taken. One threat, however, seemed less and less likely. The family was caught up in its own destruction, and word from their sources said that other groups were adding to the carnage.

Kirith hoped viciously that they all eliminated each other. He had been too long in the shadow of their revenge, and to have both he and his lover safe from that particular threat would be a great relief, perhaps even an opportunity for them to be able to travel, to see the world without fear of reprisal.

For him finally to see his mother's birthplace, Norway. He

wistfully hoped he could gift such a thing to his lover, to show him his roots.

Kirith rose and stretched, then bent to Chase. "I am going for a run with Landon. I assume you don't want to join us?"

Chase huffed, shaking his head. "This morning was enough, thanks. Run your fool heads off." Kirith could not prevent a short burst of laughter, before looking up the beach.

Landon waited, impatient.

Landon's eyes met Kirith's, and he began to make his way over, with that long, smooth stride that always got Kirith's blood up.

Sexy and powerful.

"Ready for a run?" Landon's tone held a promise.

Kirith grinned, unable to help himself at the prospect of some time alone with his lover. It had been some time since they had had privacy, or even the desire, with everything that had happened.

The stretch of muscle felt wonderful, their long strides even and steady, together in this, as with everything.

After a mile or so, they stopped, as if in synchronicity, facing the ocean for long moments, absorbing both its beauty and its power.

Landon curled his hand behind Kirith's neck, bringing him in for a deep kiss, inviting his lover's tongue out to play.

Kirith moaned in response, wrapping his arm around Landon's waist and tugging him tightly against his body, letting him feel the abrupt arousal that made Kirith's shorts far too snug.

Landon slid a hand down, rubbing Kirith's cock with knowing fingers, proficient in bringing his lover into instant hardness, murmuring soft promises in his ear.

Kirith growled, tugging Landon after him into the surf, facing the ocean. Pulling Landon's shorts down and off, flinging them toward the shore, he then set to work on his own, freeing his painful shaft with alacrity.

Landon refused to let go of him, kissing over his neck, breathing into his ear, and making Kirith shiver uncontrollably.

With a groan of need, Kirith hefted his lover, Landon wrapping his legs around Kirith's waist with ease, the water buoying his movements.

Kirith slipped into him, water aiding the cause, though Landon hissed a little. Kirith was too large to take easily without stretching. A wave washed past them, lifting Landon, moving him upon Kirith's cock. They both groaned with pleasure.

It was long, and lazy, letting the waves do the work, prolonging the heat, and the sensation, building it bit by bit.

Landon threw his head back at last, clutching at Kirith, staring blindly at the blue sky. "Fuck me. Please, now...I..."

Kirith obeyed, chasing his own orgasm with sharp thrusts that slowed with the water's resistance. He circled his hips, pinning Landon against him, holding him mercilessly in place.

Landon's mouth opened, but no sound came out, only a silent scream as he came, a sudden warmth along Kirith's abs, that almost instantly washed away.

Kirith stiffened against him, before crying out with release, Landon's name echoed by the seagulls that whirled above.

They almost collapsed then, perhaps would have, if Landon had not nimbly disentangled himself, standing in the surf and catching Kirith around the waist.

They stood, entwined, breath harsh, feeling some of the ever present grief and tension drain away, cleansed by the ocean herself.

Chase dusted the sand off his shorts, wondering how long Kirith and Landon would be gone.

Kirith had taken Chase on a similar exercise just that morning, but Chase had not enjoyed the experience. He would have a long way to go in training before he could match Kirith's fitness and endurance. Still, it would be good to work upon such a thing. The workout brought a kind of numb peace that he longed for.

He stared out to sea, his thoughts too fragmented to focus on his studies. The steady crash of the waves was soothing, the tranquility of the island working upon his shattered nerves. If only he did not feel so alone, as though a ghost sat at his side, leaving a cold void. He let his head hang, taking a deep breath. There were no more tears. He had shed them all, and the pain was now deeper than any tears could possibly express.

The faint sound of a boat motor dragged him out of his dismal thoughts and back to the present. He raised his head, noting wearily that the weekly deliveries were being made. Kirith had people on one of the larger islands who looked after their needs and sent whatever was required via boat on a weekly basis. Such things as food, supplies, mail, and an exchange of people who looked after Raymond.

Already he could see several guards striding from the main house down to the docks to meet the approaching vessel.

Chase rose to his feet and brushed off the sand with slow, absent strokes before bending to gather up his text books. Kirith had ordered him some new architectural volumes, so he was anticipating their arrival. With any luck, they would be in this week's goods, and he could while away his time with their contents, instead of hovering near Kirith like a lost soul.

He needed to become more independent again. He could not forever lean on Kirith as his emotional support. It had been six months. He needed to find his feet and stand as a man, not a frightened, grief-stricken boy. He was spending time with Raymond, trying to help him remember, to work his way back to functioning once more. How much true help he was, he did not know, but he and the other man were becoming close, something he was grateful for.

Sighing at his morose thoughts, he turned for the house,

watching the happiness down at the docks with a faint wistfulness.

Several of the guards here were from surrounding islands and therefore had family close by. They were so much warmer in manner than the other men, and Chase often sat with one or the other islander, enjoying their calm acceptance of life, their enjoyment in small things. He had learned so much, from climbing a coconut tree to fishing from the rocks on the south side of the island. They had become much needed friends and had helped him begin to heal.

The boat was run by relatives and also brought news of others. During the rotation of guards and other staff, the boat would take them home and bring others in their place. Chase always enjoyed the rich language, the love of life that seemed to come so naturally to those who had been born in this region.

He gained the sanctuary of the veranda, safe from the direct sun, and laid his work on the ornate patio table there. Trying to avoid his own thoughts, he settled back into the large chair, staring blankly at the beauty of his surroundings.

The smell of lasagna wafted from the open windows, and he sniffed appreciatively. Moments later, Ms. Granger appeared as though she had anticipated his arrival, a cool glass of lemonade brought to the table. She laid a kiss upon his forehead, smoothing his hair for a long moment, before she smiled and turned to reenter her new domain. She was so happy here, settling in better than Chase would ever have imagined. Her smiles were more frequent, and Chase had inklings that she was growing quite close to a certain islander…

Chase thanked the stars that she was here, safe, and part of the family again.

Finding a faint smile for the first time in far too long, he bent his head and returned to his studies.

Kirith and Landon looked rumpled, but satiated upon their return, and it was completely evident what they had been up to.

Chase felt a twinge of jealousy, lowering his gaze to his books. Kirith and Landon had gone through so much. They deserved their happiness.

It was worse when Kirith leaned over Chase, laying a kiss upon the top of his head and stroking back his hair.

When Chase looked up to meet those beautiful eyes, he saw nothing but sympathy and deep understanding there.

He tried to smile, but it came out more as a grimace than anything else.

They were interrupted as the Ms. Granger came out with lunch, Laura in her wake, helping as usual.

The woman fussed with the arrangement of plates, humming.

"Did you order a new houseplant, sir? One came with the boat, and I wondered if they made a mistake. It did not seem to be something you would add to your atrium."

Kirith looked up from where he was now seated, trying to fend Landon away from taking the whole bowl of potato salad for himself.

"A plant?" he asked, distractedly.

"An ivy."

Kirith dropped his plate, staring at her in disbelief, his face paling.

Chase pushed back his chair abruptly, alarm surging through him at the other man's strange reaction.

Landon supported his lover from the other side, food forgotten. "What? What's wrong?"

"It's an old signal. From way back after I killed our father. I had to remain in the house with the guards, and sometimes Enzo would be out, away for days. While he was gone, he arranged to send me snippets of ivy, a way of telling me he was fine, safe. We joked that ivy was tough to kill—like him." Kirith was almost whispering, his voice rough and cracked.

He looked up, met Chase's worried look.

"He's alive. Enzo's alive."

Chase peered out the window, watching the jungle below grow larger as they descended. He chewed his lip nervously, drawing blood again. He could not, would not, believe this was real, that his lover was alive, until he saw proof. Until he saw Enzo himself.

Kirith's firm belief, his utter faith that Enzo would be here in Peru, worried both Chase and Landon. Had it been mere chance that the ivy had arrived on the island? Kirith often ordered plants for his atrium. Was it possible that this was a mistake? And if so, what would be the effect when Kirith discovered he was wrong, that Enzo was truly dead?

Chase couldn't bear to envision such a thing. Kirith was investing everything of himself into this search, and those who loved him could only follow, praying that he was right, waiting to pick up the pieces if he was wrong.

Chase himself couldn't open to hope.

He saw his own skepticism on Landon's face, but for Kirith's sake they were silent on the matter.

Kirith was like a madman. He had spent days phoning unnamed sources, people he seemed to know, others who were obviously strangers.

Now they were flying to a small village on a whisper of information and Kirith's hope. And with them, despite all protests to the contrary, was Raymond, determined to know, to be there whether the news was grim or joyful. He was weak, but nobody could possibly talk him out of something so important.

The private jet landed gently upon the dirt airstrip, finally coming to a complete stop, the engines powering down. Brian and his men stepped out first, searching the immediate area, before they allowed the passengers off the plane.

Kirith waited with clear impatience, his eyes glinting with suppressed eagerness, his body visibly tense with the need to act, to move. When the all clear was given, Landon walked in front of his lover, eyes flicking everywhere at once, one hand always on Kirith. Several guards helped Raymond out, and he stood straighter than he had been so far, obviously determined to show no weakness to any watchers.

Chase felt his heart sink as he was finally allowed to step onto the airstrip. He could see no happy ending coming of this endeavor at all. He was far too intimately acquainted with pain and disappointment to believe in the veracity of a single, possible sign.

Part of him believed that Enzo had been taken from him because he was not worthy — that someone above had realized his true self and had seen fit to take his joy from him. After everything that had been done to him over the years, how could he possibly be someone the heavens looked upon favorably?

The sound of engines drew him from tortured musings. Guns drawn, the team surrounded Chase, Kirith, Landon, and Raymond.

Four rough-looking SUVs emerged from the jungle to their left, from a track that in no way resembled a road. There appeared to be eight well-armed men, tough and somewhat scruffy, their clothing half uniform, half camouflage. The vehicles slid to a stop, fresh mud everywhere upon their surfaces, the men themselves spotted with dirt.

Silence fell for long moments as the two groups stared at each other, the only sound the soft ticks of the cooling engines.

Finally, one of the men slid from behind the steering wheel, his movements rife with a sinuous grace that proclaimed him predator. The other men followed, gathering behind him, naming him their leader without a word being spoken.

The man approached, his stride sure and even, his cold brown eyes fixed upon them with no fear, even as the men around Chase shifted, their stances widening in warning, guns shifting higher in their grips.

Some small distance from their position, he stopped, viewing them silently, gaze trailing over each man, landing finally on Kirith. His eyes widened ever so slightly, then a smirk slid over his features, his head tilting slightly.

"My brother hadn't mentioned how beautiful you are, Kirith Martinelli. If he had, I wouldn't have waited, I would have come to fetch you myself." Those brown eyes had become heated, sliding over Kirith's body with blatant appreciation.

Landon snarled, stepping in front of his lover, bristling with tension.

Kirith put a hand upon his shoulder, holding him steady for a moment, their eyes meeting, something silent passing between them. Kirith then stepped forward, gaze cool and remote, daring the man to disrespect him further.

The man grinned, white teeth flashing against darkly tanned skin, folding his arms over his mud-spotted chest. His black hair, short cut, suited his cheeky demeanor. He was shorter than any of Kirith's people, but his attitude more than made up for it.

Kirith narrowed his eyes. "Your people told me you might know where Enzo Martinelli is. Is this true?"

Chase was proud of the tone of Kirith's voice. No one would ever know the eagerness behind it — the sheer desperation that had fuelled this flight, this pursuit of a mere rumor. Kirith stood motionless, waiting for an answer, his body giving no sign of the tension he must be feeling.

The newcomer's gaze slid from him to Landon, his smirk widening, before he bowed from the waist, with a formal precision out of place in a steaming jungle, among men such as this.

"I am Raoul Marito Mendoza."

Kirith drew a deep breath, his eyes lighting to fire.

"Santos's brother."

Raoul watched him, hunger still evident in his dark eyes. "The one and same." He smiled then, softer. "We have something of yours…"

Far from Chase's expectations, the house they arrived at was huge, enclosed in a walled, guarded area. Raoul himself showed them inside, and Chase stared in awe. The architecture seemed very old Spanish, with beautiful golden tile flooring and whitewashed walls. Raoul led them to a vast room, warm and obviously decorated for social occasions, with couches and chairs grouped intimately around the space. Fans whirred lazily over their heads, stirring the cool air. Chase cautiously seated himself on one of the expensive-looking chairs, his gaze taking in the large pieces of artwork that graced the area. There were paintings, several large sculptures both classical and modern, wall hangings with a local flavor, and at the head of the room, a water wall that provided a welcome respite from the heat outside. Over their heads, great beams, dark-stained, gave an almost medieval flavor to the decor.

Wealth was evident everywhere. Tasteful, knowledgeable wealth.

Rising once again, Chase paced, trying to breathe normally. The beauty of the house, so palatial, soon slid from his thoughts.

Santos himself, shorter than Chase had expected, but darkly powerful, strode into the room. He greeted Kirith and Raymond with obvious pleasure and then gestured them all further down a hallway.

They entered a quiet suite of rooms, and Chase was pulled into Kirith's embrace.

"Santos suggested I go in first. Are you all right with that?"

Chase could not speak, despairing thoughts crowding his mind. Of course Kirith would go first—he was more important. Who was Chase? And what if this was not Enzo? He knew that made no sense. Santos would know, but he couldn't eliminate his fears.

He only nodded. Kirith hugged him, then turned to the door that Santos held open, his expression holding both fear and hope in one package.

The door closed behind him.

Now Chase waited, so many emotions crowding in that he could make no sense of just one. If there could be a future between them. If Enzo truly cared, why would he have waited so long to tell them he was alive? Had he changed his mind about Chase, seen him clearly enough this time, not wanting him after consideration?

Kirith came out of the room with a pale face and tear tracks upon his cheeks. Chase clenched his fists, fear overwhelming him. He had been grateful that Kirith had gone inside first.

Now that the moment had arrived, when he should have been wild with impatience to see his lover, he was frozen with a strange reluctance.

Fear.

What if he was different, not wanting Chase anymore? He had lost him once. He could not bear it again. Their relationship had been so fragile, so new.

He did not understand his own emotions, as they swirled about him.

Kirith crossed over to him, through the ring of silent watchers. Taking Chase's hand in his, he squeezed, expression gentling.

"Go to him. Be prepared, Chase. He is scarred…" Kirith swallowed hard, then leaned down to hug him. "He is very weak."

Chase shivered, fingers reaching out to clench into Kirith's shirt. "Does he want to see me?" His whisper was unsteady.

"He fears what you will think, how you will view him now." Kirith shook his head at Chase's look of disbelief.

"He has ignored my scars, helped me heal, and thinks I will judge his?" Chase drew away, feeling a rising anger pushing back his fears.

Scowling, he pushed past Kirith, stalking over the door and opening it with some force. He drew a deep breath, before entering and closing it behind him with a sharp snick.

The room was dim, curtains half drawn, heavy with shadows. The large bed lay in a pool of darkness, and Chase thinned his lips, striding to the windows, and heaving back the curtains to let the sun in, before whirling to face the room's occupant.

Chase let out a gasp and he flew forward, reaching out and taking a thin hand in his, bringing it to his lips, never taking his eyes from his lover's gaunt face.

One dark eye met his, the other hidden beneath a light bandage that covered the entire right side of Enzo's face. His right arm was similarly swathed, and Chase swallowed hard, imagining the pain of burns covering so much flesh.

His gaze returned to Enzo's.

Enzo watched him, face completely void of expression, his body rigid with tension, muscles tight.

Chase tried to speak, but the silence overwhelmed him and he could only twist his fingers together, wishing desperately for eloquence.

The tension stretched, and he took another step forward, trying to force himself to action, fear rising that he would only say the wrong thing, do the wrong thing.

Enzo closed his eye, turned his face aside back into shadow.

"You should go," he said, voice hollow and hoarse. "I am alive. That is all you needed."

The words broke some barrier in Chase, and he offered a shaky smile, tears rising to his eyes, relieved he could read his lover so easily. "You are an idiot, my love. You accepted me when no one else would, and now you think I would turn from you? I love you. That is for always and forever, and no scars, no injuries are going to change that." He leaned forward and laid a trembling hand against one lean cheek. "God, I'm so sorry you were hurt. I would have been here, I would have—"

Enzo raised the hand he held and laid a finger upon his lips. That dark eye searched his, and he consciously opened himself, wanting there to be no shadows between them.

Chase kissed the digit with gentle care, afraid to do anything more, afraid to cause more pain than his lover had already endured.

Enzo's body seemed to relax a small amount, as though he had received Chase's silent message in full.

"You are a fool to love me." Enzo gave a small half smile, before grimacing with pain. "*Mi sei mancato*, my love. So much. But Sergei insisted that we wait, wanted the world to think I had died, so I did not get pulled into the Martinelli war. You and Kirith were being watched by them. We could not get word to you without giving everything away. I am so sorry."

"Sergei? He's alive?" Joy swelled inside him. He had not dared hope…

"Saved my life, the stupid bastard. Burned himself in the doing." Enzo voice was hoarse and rough, as though he had not spoken for a while.

"Then I will forgive him for keeping you hidden. I do understand his motives, but Kirith and I…" He closed his eyes at the pain of his memories. It took a moment before he could pull back from the past and move into the present, into the gift he had been given, now when he thought all hope was gone.

Chase leaned forward, laying his lips over Enzo's with a soft, soothing murmur. "I'm here. That's over."

Enzo shifted, sitting up a little, pain etching his face. Putting his left arm out, he drew Chase down upon the bed, tucking him against his side with an echo of his old strength.

"I will be nothing great to look at. The right side of my face, my right arm…Darell thought I would lose use of it completely, but it is healing better than expected. But I am never going to look like you are used to. There is no hope for my eye…"

Chase shook his head, putting his hand over Enzo's mouth. "Do you think I'm so shallow? You told me I'm strong in myself, that I can make my own decisions, yet now you think I would walk away for so little a thing? I love you. I will love your scars. I will kiss them until you accept they are part of you now, that I am beyond that. Our love is beyond that. I have never believed in perfection, never been perfect myself. Yet you took me in, showed me what it is to be accepted, loved. Now, we will be equals. I can do the same for you."

Enzo drew in a shaky breath, his control obviously paper thin. "You are so young…"

Chase sat up sharply, scowling. "If you bring out that old argument one more time, I might forget you are injured at all. Stop fighting this. I love you, damn it. And I will keep at it until you actually believe."

Enzo huffed a little, his eye showing a new, faint amusement in its weary depths. "My little tiger. As you wish then." His left hand lifted, drew Chase in for a kiss. "And when I met you, you were a mere mouse. Now a tiger. You have come a long way, my love."

"Because of you," Chase rejoined, managing a smile. "You brought me out of the darkness, lifted me up and made me believe. Now I will do that for you. We will truly be equals now."

Enzo pulled him down, resting them forehead to forehead, sharing breath.

"This is going to be a long road of healing. Are you ready for this?"

Chase felt a true smile curve his lips.

"Always."

Epilogue

They stood upon the tarmac, watching the plane taxi toward them. The wind was hot, no mercy in its touch, and Chase wiped away a bead of sweat that trickled down his temple.

Enzo looked down at him, a smile tilting one corner of his lips. He showed no sign of even realizing it was hot at all. Chase tried not to resent that.

"Perhaps you should wait in the car, with Kirith, and the others. They were sensible."

Chase scoffed. "As if. I want to be here with you. Just the two of us."

Enzo shook his head, but graced Chase with a kiss on the lips, regardless of who might be watching at the airport.

The plane taxied to its spot, powering down, the strident noise slowly dying away. Chase waited with clear impatience, almost dancing from foot to foot.

Enzo was motionless, quiet, his single dark eye fixed upon the door that slowly opened, the steps lowering.

Chase glanced at his lover again, grinning a little. The eye patch had a piratical air…damn sexy. The cool facade no longer fooled him. He knew Enzo all too well now, and he knew that the other man was as edgy as Chase himself was.

They both froze in place, as Sergei ducked out the plane's door, a bundle held carefully in his huge arms. The nurse was close behind him, concern on her face, as though she doubted Sergei's ability to care for such a precious burden.

Chase tugged on Enzo's hand, but his lover did not move. Looking at his face, Chase thought that perhaps he could not move, his body tense, his gaze fixed upon what Sergei held.

Chase subsided, curbing his own longing in favor of helping Enzo through this.

Sergei stalked up to them, a grin evident, before gently pulling back the embroidered blanket and letting them see their daughter for the first time.

Chase leaned forward eagerly, a small gasp escaping him as a tiny fist waved in the air. He wanted to touch so badly, but more than that, he wanted Enzo to have this moment, to be the first of them to hold her.

Enzo was staring at the child, his dark eye fathomless. For a moment, Chase worried.

His lover gave a huff of exasperation, perhaps at himself more than anything, and reached out. Sergei carefully transferred his charge into Enzo's grasp, watching with a fond smile as his friend held the child with expert care.

The little girl could not be in safer arms.

Chase grinned at the captain's expression, then reached out to touch soft, dark hair, wonder on his face.

"How could she give this up?" he whispered. Stacey had signed the baby over without a qualm, trading her parental rights for a large sum of money. Looking into the cherubic face of their new daughter, Chase could not imagine such a thing.

Enzo held his daughter firmly, though it had to have been causing him some pain. He had worked hard for this moment, for the ability to hold his child with both arms.

Chase was damn proud.

They heard voices approaching, Kirith, Landon, Laura, and

Raymond coming to meet the new member of the family.

Enzo leaned down, laid a kiss upon his daughter's brow.

"Tell her what her name is, my love."

Chase felt a rush of love for them both.

He stepped closer, enclosing the child between them, safe and secure.

"Abrielle," he whispered, "welcome home."

~ About the Author ~

Writing has always been of the utmost importance to me, often a means of expressing frustration, anger and grief during terrible times in my life. It was also there for the joys and triumphs, a faithful companion through it all that never failed me.

I have written over twenty books, but most of them will never see the light of day. Due to various friends urging, I realized that I should share some of these.

I now realize that I actually have stories to tell and I want to share them.

I live in Alberta, Canada, a truly beautiful place. I am grateful that I was fortunate to be born here, to know peace and prosperity in my culture. So many do not have that.

My life has been full, not perhaps with successes as today's world expects, but with so many, many experiences.

I have two sons, very large sons. My eldest is 6'4" and the youngest 6'7". They have been my life and it is wonderful to see them on their own paths, beginning their own lives. They are my strength and my pride and now I have my almost daughter in law, Kim to help keep "the boys" in line.

My partner, John, is the rock I bounce my ideas off of. He is the best of friends and a true confidante. Somehow he puts up with such a chaotic household…and ferrets. Truly an adaptable man!

So there you have it, my life in a nutshell!

I hope you enjoy my writing. It has been such an experience writing them all and they are such a reflection of my state of mind that it is intensely personal to share.

Discover more about J. C. Owens here

http://www.jcowensauthor.net

~ Also Available from J.C. Owens ~

Taken

Kidnapping the brother of a mob boss was madness. If only it had stayed that simple.

It had all gone wrong. Sent as a mercenary to kidnap Kirith Martinelli from his tropical island home, Landon finds himself on the wrong end of a job gone bad. But there's more to Kirith than meets the eye—he's the brother of feared mob boss Enzo Martinelli, and he's taken Landon as his captive. Kirith makes Landon an offer he can't refuse: stay with him for three months—until he tires of Landon's body—and then Landon may go free.

Landon, fearing his own criminal family more than the man before him, quickly agrees. Three months will buy him enough time for his brothers to lose his scent, and then freedom will be his. But that freedom has a steeper price than Landon bargained for as he's drawn into the secrets of Kirith's past. He can't ignore the sadness and loss behind his captor's beautiful eyes, and Landon finds himself wondering if three months will be enough—for either of them…

Available now in print and digital format

Lightning Source UK Ltd.
Milton Keynes UK
UKOW04f2120170315

248065UK00001B/239/P